Jalena

DANCES WITH

GOD

~Life is a beautiful dance with God~

Theresa M. Odom-Surgick

Cover created by: Donna Osborn Clark at CreationbyDonna.com

Interior design and typesetting by: interiorbookdesigns.com

DMO Music & Creative Arts Publishing

ISBN-13: 978-0615767109 (Custom)

ISBN-10: 0615767109

In memory of my parents, Benjamin Odom and Delila Melrose Jacobs

Chapter 1

"Jalena...Jalena! Wake up."

Pastor Harvey stood over Jalena Mathesin as she slept on a borrowed cot. The Greater Saint James Restoration Center was a place of refuge for Jalena. Reaching down, he tapped her on the shoulder and loudly said, "Jalena, wake up it's time to get up."

Hearing his heavy voice and feeling his touch startled her. Jalena sat straight up with hands cocked in self defense ready to protect herself.

"Hold up, Jalena. It's me." Pastor Harvey jumped back away from her.

"Pastor," she yelled. I'm so sorry." Her hands quickly came down and she rubbed her tired eyes.

"Sorry I frightened you. Did you complete your assignment?" he asked.

"What assignment?"

"Come on, Jalena. You know the assignment I'm talking about. We discussed this in great detail last night. You're over your limited stay here. We can no longer house you. The maximum amount of days per person is 90 and we've allowed you to stay 120. It's not fair to the other clients. I'm sorry, but you need to give in and go home."

Jalena looked up at Pastor Harvey with water filled eyes and said, "I tried calling her a few times. But when I hear her voice, I get nervous and hang up without saying a word. I feel as if phoning her is taking the coward's way out. Talking to her face-to-face would be better, so I can see the expression on her face when I talk to her. I want Mom to see me and see who I've become. My messy life is over. I'm not the same person who left that night, and I'll never be that person again as long as I have breath in my body."

"Jalena, I believe you. But now it's up to you. Go home and let your mother know about your turn around. If you don't want to talk to her on the phone go...go and tell her. But, you can't stay here another night. You have to go. I'm sorry. I'm getting too many complaints from other clients to my staff members. They're wondering why I'm giving you so much leeway. I can't have people going to upper leadership and complaining. I'll lose my job. So do what you have to do. 5 o'clock is the deadline."

Pastor Harvey was sad. He felt the pain she was feeling, but there was no longer anything he could do about it. He was being pressured. This would be her final day. He felt bad for Jalena, but as Director of Placement, he was the youngest pastor to ever be given a job of this magnitude and didn't want to jeopardize his position.

"Let me know if you need anything else," he said as he sadly walked away. Stopping in his tracks, he turned back to her and said, "I made a call to Liberty Housing. Pastor Jackie said you're welcome to stay there if needed." He walked away.

Jalena was trembling inside. Tears rolled down her cheeks as her mind revisited her past – a dark place of anguish and painful memories. It took months for the haunting screams she could only imagine coming from her mother to subside. Because she was not there, it was all left to the imagination. Jalena was to blame. *If only I could turn back the hands of time and do it all over - things would be different,* she thought.

Life had handed Jalena some good times and sadly, some tumultuous. There was no one to blame but herself. Sitting on the cot, she thought about her old life. Good friends were lost when she started hanging around with the gang. She was angry at life and took it out on her family and friends by turning her back on them.

Prior to all this, Jalena was a nice family oriented girl. She worked as a receptionist at a dry cleaning establishment. Jalena worked hard, catering to everyone she met, greeting each one with a smile. But then one day she met MD – Moses Dorin. He was called MD not only because of the initials in his name, but also for what they stood for in another meaningful term: medical doctor. This MD always had whatever anyone needed for whatever pain they had. Whatever the issue, MD had the means to fix it for you.

On the streets, he was also known as the medicine man. Just like Moses in the Bible, Moses Dorin could lead anyone to the Promised Land with his pocketful of miracle drugs. Jalena's first encounter with MD was at the cleaners. Her dad had recently passed and she was in tremendous emotional and mental pain.

Since Moses was a regular customer, she and MD would frequently engage in conversations. Jalena got to know him pretty well and trusted MD. They became friends. That's when he offered her his free "medical" help. He told Jalena that it would relieve the pain of her dad's loss.

Arrangements were made. His plan was to meet her at his friend's house. He'd be hanging out with a few of his buddies. So Jalena went there and before she knew it, she was flying high. All the pain and heartache she felt had temporarily been erased from her mind.

The feeling of missing her dad was sometimes unbearable. He was her buddy, but now he was gone. With MD's help, she found solace in the feeling she got when high. MD was her savior as she lay there, limp as a rag doll. Some nights, when she was high, he would secretly mess with her body. Jalena was not a virgin, so she had no idea when things happened to her. MD would clean her up when he finished his business.

Her mother was oblivious to what was happening to her daughter. At night, when Jalena returned home, she went straight up to her room and hid until the next day. Her family was blind to the emotional stress and depression that was caused due to the death. She was now delving deeply into drugs. Both her mom and Jared, her brother, thought Jalena was just extremely tired from going to school and then straight to work each day.

She'd sleep off the high and be right back at it the very next day. Most times, Jalena faked going to school. She was handing in homework assignments that were gleaned from loyal friends and then sit in class when she felt like it. There were no calls to home from school administration to inform her mother of the delinquency, so Jalena did what she wanted without fear of repercussion. More often than not, she skipped school and headed over to the "Hideout" - a place where her new friends gathered each day.

The night before the incident at her mother's house, Jalena was with them and talked a little too much. She bragged about her dad's expensive watches. She even mentioned where they were kept in the house. The next thing she knew, they were making plans as to how to get them and how much money they'd sell for. She tried stopping them, but had no influence. They wouldn't listen.

She wasn't an official member of the gang, but because of her constant presence, they thought of her as one of the family. They called her Little Sis. She loved it. Jalena felt like she belonged; they were her family. Everyone made her feel good and so did MD with his miracle meds. She was truly in love with the feeling. It became her friend. Meds were like candy to her, so they gave Jalena just what she needed. In order to shut her up and stop any attempts at getting what they wanted from her mom's home, they drugged her. There was a desperation to stop any plans made, but Jalena was so high that she slept until the next day. She never made it home until everything was over and done with.

During the perpetration of the crime, someone mentioned her name. They talked about Jalena. She knew it because when she returned home the next day, her brother Jared was livid and threw her up against the wall, telling her everything that was said. He yelled in her face explosively, with expletives she'd never knew could come from her brothers mouth. He angrily revealed what happened and stated that if he hadn't come in when he did, my Mom might have been killed. He then proceeded to tell Jalena to take anything she needed and leave their home.

Screaming at her he said, "Dammit, Jalena. You're going to learn the hard way. Since you love the streets so much, get your things and go. Get out of here. Get out now."

At first she thought her brother was kidding. Jalena strained hard apologizing, but he wouldn't hear her.

He interrupted her every word and said, "The safety of my mom comes first. You're not going to put us in harm's way anymore. It's time for you to make up your mind as to what you're going to do. You love the streets, so go live on the streets with your buddies! Get your stuff. Get whatever you need and get out of here now."

Jalena stood there hurt and softly said, "She's my mom too."

As she finished those few words, Marinda, her mother, slowly walked down the stairs and didn't say a word as she blankly stared at Jalena.

Nervously Jalena said, "Mom, are you alright?"

Marinda never answered her daughter. Sadness marked her swollen eyes while each bruise on her face and arms told the story of the pain and physical brutality she endured during the break in. Marinda Mathesin rejected Jalena's advances at showing concern and turned away from her daughter. There was nothing more Jalena could say or her mother wanted to hear. Jared was now in charge.

"Mom?" Jalena yelled and took a step towards her mother, but then Jared threatening her said, "If you don't leave right now, I'm calling the police. You just better be glad that Mom refuses to press any charges against you. Test me and you'll see my wrath. No longer will you stay here and threaten our safety. Get out before I call the cops," he harshly said.

Jalena was hurt, but knew it was best that she leave. Confusion hit hard as she turned and walked towards the door. Discombobulated, she thought, *How could this be happening? What was I thinking?* After she left, Jalena stopped by the police station and gave names of all the gang members. Arrests were made that same night.

Now, here she sat on a used cot in a place that had become her new haven of rest, but was now being asked to leave there too. Jalena packed what little she had and walked out thinking of her next move.

Chapter 2

As she carefully stepped between two large oak trees, Jalena stood staring at the house. Evicted, she no longer called it home. Beautiful Christmas decorations were placed around each window. Wreaths, lights and tall Angels stood blowing trumpets. They covered each side of the snow covered lawn. With eyes filled with tears, she felt emotional. It used to be home - a place of happiness and love, but shattered due to her selfish defiance which she allowed to stand in the way. With heart throbbing, she slowly stepped along the cobblestone walkway and rang the doorbell. Jalena waited.

Anxiously she thought, *Where is she?* Jalena then knocked on the door. *What's taking her so long? Is she here? God, please let Mom be home and don't let her turn me away.*

Please! She has to be home! I need to talk to her. Please, God! Please?

Marinda, Jalena's mom, opened the door. Standing there, she didn't say a word. She just stared at Jalena with no emotion or sign of pleasure in seeing her own daughter. Before having a chance to slam the door shut, Jalena blurted out, "Mom, please...please forgive me. Don't shut me out again. Please give me another chance and listen to what I've come to say. I'm so sorry for everything that I put you through. I've changed. I really have. Every day at lunch time, I attend the Greater Saint James Restoration Center listening to Pastor Harvey. I'm going to individual counseling and it's helped me to release my anger and bitterness."

Jalena was talking fast. This moment in time was a manifestation of dreams. She didn't want to lose her words or the opportunity to say all she felt.

"I'm putting God first in my life, Mom. I'm no longer in denial. The things I did were grave mistakes, and I recognize it without a shadow of doubt. Really—I do. I know I can't change my past and all the horrible things I did. I was blaming it all on the death of daddy. I was filled with so much hurt and depression and I wasn't able to let go of the grief I was feeling. But now I have. I also know that I can't let my difficult past dictate my future and all that God has planned for my life. So Mom, please believe me even if you can't totally trust me yet. I want to come back home. I need you. I love you, and I'm sorry from the depths of my heart for everything that I've done to hurt you and Jared. This family is more important than ever. I want my place back in your heart and in this home."

Jalena stood there pleading her case and defending her cause like a common criminal before her judge and jury. It was hard to tell what Marinda was thinking and feeling. Jalena completed her assignment and stood there waiting for a clear response. She knew in her heart that her mother would never stop loving her no matter how hard she tried, but there remained scars yet to be healed.

Suddenly, Jalena felt light headed and weak. As she began to slump down, Marinda caught her daughter and prevented her from hitting the concrete stairs. She yelled for Jared's help. Love prevailed as Marinda hugged her child tightly and said, "Jalena, I forgive you, baby. I forgive you."

Three little words were all that Jalena needed and wanted to hear. "I forgive you." It changed the course of her life. Once again she felt the warmth and touch of her mother. Jalena was in her arms. After all she had done, her mom had forgiven and embraced her with love. Overwhelming joy penetrated her heart – a joy that couldn't be compared to any other joy she'd ever known.

With enraptured love, Jalena knew that it was a sign from God. She was forgiven. Peace reigned in her heart. Finally, she was there in the safety of her mother's love, in her home and in her heart.

Later that evening, she was treated to her favorite meal of fried chicken, macaroni and cheese, collard green and yams followed with a hot bubbly bath. Jalena was weak and tired. Sleeping and slumbering for the next few days, her strength was renewed as Marinda nursed her back to life. It was a Christmas present that both would never forget. God answered prayer. The tragedy of her past was now buried in the sands of time.

Chapter 3

Winter had come and gone. Things had changed in the Mathesin household. Going to church every Sunday was a priority. Jalena went, received the word, studied it and was convinced of God's love. But, there were still unanswered questions and concerns. Did she really trust and believe God? It was another story when it came to applying the word to her life.

She'd grown up in the church and knew what was expected. She lifted her hands in praise, sang the songs and did the dance on one or more occasions, but when the altar call was given, she didn't want emotions to play any part in what she felt. She had to be sure it was the leading of God and His desired will for her life. Each time the invitation for discipleship was given, her mom, Marinda prayed. With head bowed and hands clasped, she implored God to move Jalena from her seat and step to the altar.

At the end of the day, Marinda would often ask her daughter, "Jalena, when will you go to the altar to give your hand to the Pastor and your heart to God?"

Frustrated, but respectfully Jalena would say, "I'm going to do it, Mom. I'm just not ready for this. Please give me a chance to settle everything in my mind. Please, Mom. I need more time."

Eventually, Marinda stopped asking. She knew this important decision was ultimately Jalena's choice to make. Besides, it made her happy seeing her baby girl attending the New Hope Missionary Baptist Church every Sunday. It was their family's church. The teachings were in them and in their home - built on legacy. Marinda's great great grandfather, Bishop Algue Jacobs, was the founder and pastor of New Hope.

Prayers had finally been answered. Marinda and Jalena attended the revival at one of the local churches. On the third night, which was the closing night of the revival, the service was remarkably different from the last two nights. There was something that had changed in the atmosphere...a soothing peace and joy that couldn't be denied.

The guest revivalist, Evangelist G.J. Townsend preached a powerful message titled "Restoration Revelation". As he ended his sermon, the choir sang a selection of invitation. Jalena listened to the harmonic voices and something stirred deep within her heart that moved within the very core of her being. Tears streamed down her face like never before as she listened to the lyrics, *You are the source of my strength. You are the strength of my life. I lift my hands in total praise to You.* The music and the lyrics permeated the atmosphere, causing an unusual worship experience to flood the sanctuary.

As much as she tried, Jalena couldn't help herself. Pure praise and worship flowed from her lips, as she lifted her hands surrendering with abandonment to the feeling deep within. Speaking in tongues, the fire of the Holy Spirit fell upon her. It was a new level in Christ – something she had never, ever felt before.

Suddenly, without hesitation, she stood and stepped out into the long, narrow aisle. Jalena felt as if she was being pulled forward by an invisible force and was no longer in control – God had this. A great flood of tears and a wailing cry welled up deep within. Unable to hold back, the cries she needed to release came bursting forth from her lips. A ministry leader rushed up to her side and helped Jalena make her way towards Pastor Gregory Boyd who stood at the altar with hands lifted high. He was ready to accept those who made it up to the altar. It was at that moment that Jalena rededicated her life to Christ.

It was a high time. People in the congregation lifted up a great and mighty outpouring of thunderous praise all around her. Some were shouting and others were crying. The sanctuary was filled with uninhibited praise and worship. Her knees felt wobbly and blinding tears burned Jalena's eyes, so much so that at one point, she felt as if she'd seen a fog-like cloud pass through as the choir continued to lift up the song of praise. It felt as if God's Shekinah presence had overtaken and inhabited the sanctuary.

This was it. Fervent, effectual prayers had prevailed. After taking that much anticipated walk down the aisle and publicly proclaiming her faith, Jalena gave her life back to Christ. It was overwhelming. The finality of all she had been through and the knowledge of how far she had come became crystal clear. When her mother ran up and embraced her, it was at that moment Jalena knew in her heart that everything was finalized—it was now official. Everything had changed—nothing was the same and true forgiveness had just taken place.

<><><>

A sleepless night followed. Many unanswered questions raced back and forth in Jalena's mind. She sat in the living room, praying and asking God questions.

"What happened? What is this? And who are You?"

Even though she was born and raised in this Christian household, there were still a myriad of questions about the ways of God and who He was.

"Why are You doing this to me? What have I done for You that caused You to make me feel this way? Why? I'm not worthy of anything that You have for me. I've been too mean and too hurtful to others, especially to myself and to my family. So why would You even care this much for me? Please answer me?" Jalena was now in tears.

"I need an answer from You. I need clarity. Please?"

"Jalena? Are you all right? Who were you talking to?"

Standing there, her mother interrupted the quiet time and inquisition before she could get the answers that were needed. Jalena hid her face and wiped away the welled up tears that were now falling.

She answered and said, "No one, Mom. I was just talking to myself. I'm so confused."

Marinda was concerned and said, "Confused about what, Jalena?"

Jalena paused to gather herself and to get her emotions under control. Turning to her mother she said, "I'm just overwhelmed by what happened at the church last night. You were there. You saw. What was that? What am I to do now? I feel so different inside. It's something that I've never felt before and I know that something has changed deep inside of me. Mom, I don't know how to handle these feelings. What am I supposed to do now?"

With water filled eyes, Marinda said, "Baby, I can't even speak right now without tearing up. For so long, I've prayed and prayed asking God to touch the hearts of my children. Wanting Him to change your lives and let you feel what I feel. It's real, child. It's real. What you feel is God's spirit moving in your heart. For a long time, Satan held you down. He controlled you, using you in any way he saw fit because you allowed him. But now, because you've made the choice to finally reject and resist him, he has to flee. He can no longer control you or your emotions. He can no longer hold onto you. Why? Because you gave in to God. You gave everything back to Christ."

Jalena squirmed on the couch. She didn't know how to react to her mother's words. Standing, she walked over to a window filled with plants and perennial flowers. Jalena stared out at the manicured landscape which surrounded their home that was once owned by her grandmother. She heard what her mother said, but still had a bit of confusion racing back and forth in the recesses of her mind.

"I'm so confused. This feeling is overwhelming. I know that God has changed my life, but it seems like every day I'm fighting a battle to stay free from the worldly pleasures that are constantly calling my name. I'm afraid those things and feelings are going to keep returning. They're always haunting me. I've tried hard to change the way I used to be and how I used to live. I don't want to go back and revisit that place. I don't want to ever feel that way again. Never again. Since last night, for the first time in a long time, I feel free inside. I don't have those feelings of hatred and loneliness pent up anymore. I don't feel depressed and anxious, and it happened in one night. I...I just—"

Interrupting, Marinda said, "Jalena, it didn't just happen in one night. God has been working on this plan for a long time. You were just so resistant you couldn't acknowledge what was happening. Even when you were just a child singing in the youth choir, it was prophesied that you were a special child and that one day you would perform great works and you'd be someone people could look up to."

Marinda walked over to Jalena, took her by the shoulders and gently turned her around. Now facing her daughter, Marinda continued, "Yes, you've been through a lot, but everything you've been through are the vicissitudes of life. Those tests you've gone through are now material for your powerful testimony to others who are going through quandaries in their lives. That testimony is your victory. It'll show others that just as you came through, they too can have victory."

Jalena surrendered to her tears, letting them flow freely. Marinda took Jalena's hand and they sat down on the padded window seat. She picked up her Bible, flipping through the tattered pages, and said, "Mmm... Here it is. This is the scripture that always helps me when I'm feeling confused and need God's protection over my mind and my heart. It's Psalm 91. It always makes me feel better to know that my Father God is watching, hearing and protecting in every aspect of my life."

Jalena listened intently as her mother softly read the entire passage.

Reading the last line to her daughter, Marinda then embraced Jalena and said, "Baby, always keep God's word with you. He's your protection. Pray – He will answer you. It's just that simple. Don't question Him, trying to figure out everything at once. In His time, you'll know with clarity everything He wants you to know. For now, just rest in His word, peace and presence. It's going to be okay."

"Thank you, Mom. Thank you."

Marinda kissed Jalena on the forehead.

"Don't thank me, child. I just want happiness and God's pure joy for you. I love you, baby girl."

Marinda left the house knowing that her daughter would be just fine. Jalena felt a quiet inner peace and was no longer confused. Things were going to get better and she knew it.

Chapter 4

The weekend was over and Jalena was back at work. She was feeling good as she walked into the office dressed in a gray, two-piece suit. She was ready for a productive day. Talking to her mom before getting there helped to put things in perspective. With that, there was a great expectation of how the rest of her day would transpire.

Arriving at her cubicle, Jalena smiled and greeted her co-worker. "Good morning, Laurie."

"Hey, Jalena. How was your weekend?"

She hesitated to answer. Laurie, her co-worker was the kind of person who loved to spread a little gossip. It didn't matter how menial it was, Laurie spread it. Around the office, she was nicknamed progossiper - short for professional gossiper. Most people ignored her elaborate tales, while some enjoyed and hung onto every word she concocted. Sometimes this was also their way of verifying office whisperings.

The weekend had stirred up a lot of emotion and personally, Jalena didn't care who knew or how they felt about it. Yet, she decided to hold back when answering Laurie. This tactic would slow down the headline news from making its way around the office.

She unlocked her desk and began removing a few files that needed her attention. Feeling Laurie's eyes piercing her, she looked up and said, "What?"

Cocking her head to the side, Laurie said, "How was your weekend?"

Jalena smiled faintly and said, "Why don't you tell me about yours first."

Sighing, Laurie said, "Come on, girl! I asked first. So tell me."

Jalena sensed the agitation and said, "Okay...okay, Laurie. Well...about my weekend...well, it was unusual to say the least." She paused as she threw a sheet of paper into the shredding machine and then said, "I went to church with my mom and—"

Before she could finish, the phone on her desk rang. "Peters, Simon and Jacobs. This is Jalena. May I help you? One moment, Mrs. Carr, I'll transfer your call to Mr. Jacobs."

As she transferred the call, her boss, Mr. Jonathan Peters, entered the office with a file folder protruding under his arm. He was a handsome man who presented himself in a meticulous manner. Polished shoes matched his custom-made suits, ties and pocket squares. It was very rare not to see him accessorized completely, even down to his ritzy gold cuff links which adorned his French cuffed dress shirts. Each shirt was embroidered with his initials in script on the right cuff.

The women staffers, with the exception of Jalena, swooned over him. At times, she thought it was due to the strong scent of his custom made cologne. There were times it made her sneeze. Jalena didn't think he was all that and couldn't figure out what all of the hoopla was about. He was a normal looking man. She never took a second look at him and somehow surmised he knew because it seemed he would give her a lot of time consuming work as punishment.

"Good morning, Mr. Peters. How was your weekend?" said Jalena.

His suavities and delay in answering anyone had become his modus operandi. It was an important part of who he was and his personal swag. Everyone was used to this demeanor and learned how to wait.

Flipping through single pages of a manila file folder, he casually answered, "It was okay. Just a regular weekend. Can't complain. Did a little golfing and cruising in my Jaguars. How was yours?"

Jalena sat there wondering if she should fudge her answer to him. He was a man who doubted the existence of God and was critical of those who believed in divinity. She decided to be up front with him and bear any consequences. Jalena prepared her heart and answered truthfully.

"It was quite different for me," she said.

"What made it so different?" he inquired with a hint of sarcasm.

She paused before answering to gather her thoughts, and then said, "I went to church with my mom."

With squinted eyes, he looked up from the file he held in hand, with obvious disdain.

Jonathan Peters did not hold back.

"You're kidding me, aren't you? What caused you to do that? Don't tell me you're becoming one of those Bible toting radical, saved and sanctified, Holy Roller, Christian women?"

Jalena was well prepared for his response and answered without hesitation. "Mr. Peters, I've been going to church on a regular basis. This is not the first time, it's just that this time was completely different. It was an amazing experience. Something happened to me, and it's difficult for me to even begin explaining."

Before she could say another word, he raised his voice and said, "Listen, Ms. Mathesin, don't even begin explaining. Keep your Bible story to yourself. I don't want to hear about your divine revelation and miracle working intervention. We have too much work to do here. Just make sure you don't bring any of that Jesus mess up here in this building. I'm serious when I say this. You got me?"

Undeterred by his comments, Jalena looked him in the face and said, "Yes, Mr. Peters, I got you." She quickly began organizing the folders he carelessly threw on her desk as he made a quick exit.

Checking to see that he was gone, Laurie rushed over to Jalena hoping to get more information about her weekend at church. "I'll listen. Tell me? So you went to church, huh? And...?"

After dealing with Mr. Peter's bilious attitude, Jalena didn't feel like feeding Laurie's hunger for gossip.

"And...?" Laurie repeated.

She was getting on Jalena's nerves. A day that started out good was now ruined by Mr. Peters. All she wanted now was for the questioning to end and to get started with her day. So she settled Laurie's curiosity.

"Yes, Laurie, I went to church."

"And?"

Laurie seemed to be a bit more agitated with the Jalena's hesitation.

"Come on, Jalena - What happened?"

Jalena needed to get back to work before Mr. Peters returned or one of his associates suddenly appeared out of nowhere. Sighing deeply, she began talking as quickly as possible trying to get the information out in as little time as possible.

"Yes, I went to church this weekend with my mom and something happened. I felt something so strong, wonderful and powerful. I can't even begin to explain it. All I know is something came over me. I cried like a baby and then I felt this awesome peace. It was such a warm, wonderful feeling. And you know what? This may sound crazy, but I have no desire to do some of the things I used to do. Crazy, right?"

Jalena was asking Laurie questions within the framework of her explanation, but was never really looking for a response. She continued talking away as if in a race to get to the finish line ending the conversation.

"All I know is I feel different and want to stay that way. That excitement for club hopping is gone. The desire for my Tequila is gone and—"

"Tequila...no Tequila!"

This one thing sent Laurie into a tizzy. A fire ignited within her. She jumped up, almost tripping over the waste basket and felt Jalena's forehead.

A nervous twitch was heard in her voice as she said, "No...no no...No, Jalena. You must be sick. Something's definitely wrong with you. Did you stumble and fall hitting your head on concrete or something? Girl, this just ain't you. Something's not right! You can't be talking that way. No clubs...no Tequila? Your favorite drink?

Come on, now! You're getting a checkup! I'm taking you to medical right away!"

Jalena wasn't sure if Laurie was making fun of her or if she was actually serious.

At that point, Jalena got terribly annoyed with her, especially when Laurie boldly grabbed her by the arm and said, "Let's go."

Jalena pulled back and yelled, "Get your hands off of me, Laurie. I'm just fine. I've never felt better."

Laurie released her, but continued the razzing. "You have got to be kidding me. You've got to be sick. Okay, where's the hidden camera in here? You're pulling a prank on me. Come on, Jalena, stop this. Please?"

Jalena was tired of her doubting, critical words, so with a firm, determined attitude she let Laurie know that it had to stop once and for all.

"Laurie, I am not kidding you. I'm serious and getting tired of your belittling what happened to me."

Finally sensing that Jalena was serious, Laurie took a step back and said, "Oh...my...goodness. You're serious."

"Yes, I am. I really don't know what it is, but I am not the same. I feel so different deep inside. It feels so strange." A lone tear dropped to her cheek.

As she wiped it away, she said. "You know, Laurie, when I was a child, my mother read stories about Jesus from the Bible. When I got old enough, I no longer wanted to hear about it and turned a deaf ear to her. She would tell us how Jesus healed the sick and raise the dead. Miracles happened even when He blessed bread. I had a hard time believing all of those stories she told me. I felt like they were just fairy tales and never really believed they were true. I don't know what this is I'm feeling, Laurie, but I know it has to be God. There's no other explanation. Just trust my word when I say that I'm not the same person that sat at this desk in this office last week."

With acceptance setting in, Laurie walked away shaking her head and said, "Wow, this is really something else. I am totally undone by all of this."

Jalena was now able to crack a smile. She was glad her phone rang. The conversation with Laurie ended and she really had nothing more to say on the subject. She needed to get some work completed before Mr. Peters returned.

"Peters, Simon and Jacobs. This is Jalena. How may I help you? Who is this? Tahlia! Hey, what's up? Lunch? What time? Okay, I'll meet you in the upper concourse lunchroom at 12:30 sharp. Make sure Sharina is on time? Okay, see you then."

Chapter 5

J alena and her friend Tahlia Winsome were all set and
ready to eat, but Sharina was late for lunch again, as
usual.

Tahlia was getting impatient and said, "Where on
earth is Sharina? She said she'd be on time. She hates it
whenever people start eating before she gets to the table,
but then again, that woman is never on time. She better
hurry up. My burger and fried onions are calling out my
name. Can you hear them calling me, Jalena?"

She began singing, "Tahlia...Tahlia, come on and eat
us. Whatcha waiting for...we're catching a cold."

"You are too funny," laughed Jalena. Pointing her
fork in Sharina's direction, she said, "Here she comes —
finally."

Shaking her head, Tahlia called out to Sharina and said, "Come on now! We're gonna start without you. Chop, chop."

"You know I'm picky when it comes to my food," Sharina said without apology. Her southern accent clearly resonated as she carefully placed her tray on the table and slid into the folding chair. Side eyeing each other, Tahlia and Jalena burst into laughter.

"What? What's so funny?" Sharina asked.

"Don't act like you don't know," said Jalena.

"Seriously? I have no clue what you two are laughing at," she said with hints of irritability.

Still laughing, Tahlia broke in and said, "Sharina, you know good and well you were over at the baked potato station flirting with Melvin, the cook. The minute he sees you, that young man gets to quaking in his cowboy boots. He can't even hold onto his utensils. He drops them all over the place. Melvin sees you and starts stuttering over every word...cannot get a word out. His entire demeanor changes—you know you're the cause of that. Poor Melvin." With that, the three of them laughed uncontrollably.

"Okay, okay, I'll admit it. I flirt—I do. But, there's a method to my madness. Listen, every time I look straight into his big, brown eyes, yes... he gets nervous and I get the freshest and largest looking potato. I talk about how good he is at making potatoes and while I'm building him up, he adds a little extra love and care to that big bud when he dresses it with some extra meat and veggies...ooh, and the cheese...yum yum. He prepares it just the way I like it - thank you."

In a sexy voice, Jalena softly said, "Ooh, girl...sounds kinda intimate to me."

They broke out in more laughter.

Composing herself, Tahlia said, "Sharina, you should watch that kind of stuff. Your man may find out and get awfully upset and jealous."

"What man? I don't have a man. I am single and as free as I want to be at this moment in time. The only man I truly have an everlasting affair with is God my Father?" She smiled.

Tahlia wiped away tears of laughter and said, "Come on, Sharina. You know Pastor Gregory has eyes for you."

"He does not. Why do you keep making such innuendos, Tahlia? He's never said a thing to me and has never ever indicated any such thing. It's unfathomable so stop being ridiculous."

Tahlia cocked her head and confidently said, "And do you think he will ever admit such a thing publicly? He's the pastor of a well known church. He can't have his name out there like that even though people are already talking. I heard it myself in the choir room just last week."

"Oh, no. They've been gossiping about me in the choir room – behind my back," shrieked Sharina.

"Lower your voice and calm down, girl, it's not a bad thing. Now look, Sharina, you're being too sensitive about this. You can ask certain people at church, and in unison they'll tell you the same thing. You are Pastor's fair maiden, and he wants to be your adorable prince. One day when Pastor Gregory gets bold enough, he's going to come riding up the church aisle up on a big, white stallion and ask for your hand in marriage. Mark my words, Sharina Michelle Oliver. You just mark my words. I've seen the way he spies you out when no one is looking."

Finishing up the last bit of lettuce on her plate, Jalena chimed in saying, "Ooh...you've got your pastor lusting after you."

Sharina let out a big sigh, and said, "Okay, okay, ladies. Enough already. I don't believe it. It's not true, so end it now. Let's just eat our food. We've already wasted twenty minutes of our lunch time on idle chatter."

"Whatever," said Tahlia.

After taking a few big bites of her potato, Sharina asked Jalena about her experience at the revival service.

"So, Jalena, I heard that you and momma Marinda were at revival at our church. I wanted to be there so bad, but work had me held up. I'm sorry I missed you."

"Yes, we were there. I guess you heard what happened to me?"

"Yes, I did, and I'm happy for you. Your mom has been praying about this for some time. God has finally answered her prayers."

Reflecting on that moment and on the seriousness of what happened, Jalena told them how powerful and overwhelming it was. "One minute I'm standing there listening to the choir, and the next thing I knew, I was crying and making my way down that long aisle. It felt as if someone was pulling and escorting me straight to the front of that altar. A peace that I haven't felt in years overcame me. I still don't understand what happened. It was like an out-of-body experience that can't be explained."

Shaking her head, Tahlia softly said, "Jalena, my friend, that was the Spirit of God moving and directing you, giving you His perfect peace."

Sharina then asked, "How are you feeling about all that happened?"

"You know, I'm feeling pretty good. I still have a lot of unsettled questions floating back and forth in my mind. I've got a lot of Bible studying to do. You'd think growing up in our household that I'd be cool with all this stuff. But I'm not. All of these years I've been leaning on my mom's faith and not standing on my own two feet. There's a lot of confusion racing in my mind."

"Jalena," said Tahlia, "You've always been the perpetual book worm, but some of those answers will only come through prayer and listening for the voice of God. We just want you to know that we're here for you if you ever need to talk about anything at all. Okay?" Sharina nodded in agreement.

Jalena 's eyes quickly filled with tears.

Tahlia grabbed a napkin, handed it to Jalena and said, "Oh no, don't you start the waterworks. We have to get back to work and I don't have my makeup case with me. I refuse to walk back into that office with raccoon eyes."

"I can't help it," said Jalena wiping her eyes. "Lately, all I do is cry. I've been so emotional. I love you, guys. I know I can always count on you to be there for me. Can't ask for a better support team."

Sharina stood with her tray in hand and said, "Well, ladies. It's been nice, but we better head back to work or we'll all be standing in the unemployment line or in the park singing for food."

They hugged each other and went their separate ways.

Chapter 6

I t was a long and stressful day. All Jalena wanted was to get home, relax and have some quiet time alone. It wasn't going to happen quite that way. Her cousin, Sasha, dropped in for a visit. Jalena was tired but glad to see her waiting there.

Standing in the kitchen doorway, she watched Sasha and remembered the day her Aunt Jessie adopted and brought Sasha home. She was a shy child who wouldn't talk to anyone. Sasha kept to herself and seemed fearful when anyone tried talking to or embracing her.

At the time, Jessie worked for Child Protective Services and later left that job to work with the Maryland Department of Education. Sasha was the last case that Jessie Whitehead had at that institution. Investigating Sasha's case, she fell in love with the little girl. When she found out that Sasha was up for adoption, she took immediate action to make the child an important part of her life.

Jessie told Jalena how five-year-old Sasha was found at home alone with no food or clothing. An article appeared in the local newspaper. Jessie was interviewed.

By Richard MeTada, News 3, DC:

"It hurt my heart so bad to hear that baby crying on that hot summer day. I went and picked her up from the neighbor's apartment. In the apartment where she was found, it was hotter than a blast furnace in that apartment. Little Sasha was sitting there in nothing but panties with sweat rolling down her entire body. Her underwear was soaked as if she had wet herself. Poor child. Her mother, Sandra, left a note saying that she no longer wanted to raise a child that she never wanted in the first place."

Tears welled up in Ms. Jessie Whitehead's eyes as she revealed this in our report.

Our investigation revealed that the child's mother, Sandra Norris had been a victim of rape and incest. She lived a harsh life that was filled with turmoil which landed her in prison for two years for killing a man. That man, Sandra's father, had raped her repeatedly. And when the girl told her mother about the rape, her own mother didn't believe her daughter. Sandra ended up pregnant by her rapist. Eventually, a positive DNA test showed that he indeed was the father. That's when her mother no choice but to believe her daughter. She then put him out of her home. By then, it was too little, too late. An apology couldn't heal the pain Sandra Norris had endured.

Our investigation also uncovered that the perpetrator of this crime was never arrested. Apparently, Sandra's mother pressured her into keeping quiet, saying that it was too late to press charges. We now know that it would have been better if she had gone ahead and sought justice. Maybe things would not have evolved the way they did.

Ms. Norris could not handle the thought that he was getting away with his crime, so she took Sasha, who was three at the time, to her mother's home, left and went to the rapist home and shot him dead – one bullet in the groin and one in the head."

Ms. Whitehead said, "I don't blame her for the way she felt, but there had to be another way other than killing that man. There just had to be."

The court had mercy on Sasha. They charged her with the crime but gave her a lighter sentence predicated on the knowledge that she had been raped by the man and was mentally affected by what he did to her for all of those years. They also told her that she would have to go through a year of counseling sessions and report back monthly to the court system before she was released from probation and get custody of her child.

We are now sad to report that the day Sandra Norris left her child home alone was the last day she was seen. Child

Protection Services tried finding her leaving messages with family and friends. It was even reported to the police but to no avail. Days later, Ms. Norris body was found behind a trash bin in an alley, dead from a drug overdose with the needle still clutched in her hand. Her daughter, Sasha is now in the custody of Ms. Whitehead.

<><><>

This memory was heartbreaking to Jalena. It brought back the harshness of life that Sasha endured. Sasha's case was a day-to-day ordeal for her Aunt Jessie and caused her attachment to Sasha. Feelings of love for Sasha were overwhelming. She felt so bad for the child. It was around the time when Jessie was leaving for her new job that they said Sasha was going to be put up for adoption. Jessie jumped right at the chance to adopt her. Many obstacles tried to cross her path, but Jessie never let that stop her.

When Jalena heard about the adoption, she asked her Aunt, "But what about Sasha's grandmother and other family members? How were you able to adopt knowing that she already has family?"

Jessie sat down holding a picture of Sasha in her hand and said, "When approached about taking Sasha in, her grandmother refused, saying she didn't want her because of all the hell her daughter had put them through. She felt that Sasha would only be a reminder of nothing but bad memories in her household. She said, 'I do not want that bastard child in my house or even near me.'"

Filled with anguish, Jalena was saddened. "How could she reject her grandbaby just like that? It's so sad, so sad, Aunt Jessie."

"I don't know, Jalena, I just don't know." Jessie and Jalena comforted each other.

Thinking back on that conversation brought tears to Jalena's eyes. She thanked God that although her cousin had endured much as a child, she had learned much from it and grew up to be a smart, polite and energetic young person. She was loved by all.

Breaking her thoughts away from the past, Jalena said, "Hey, Sasha. I see you're putting that key Mom gave you to good use. How's my little cousin doing today?" Embracing her, Jalena sat down beside Sasha on the sofa where she was finishing homework.

"I'm good. Just thought I'd stop by for a minute. Mom's working late again, and I didn't feel like going home just yet. Where's Aunt Marinda?"

"Well, when I left this morning, she was on her way over to Ms. Helena's to help with funeral arrangements."

"Funeral arrangements? Who died?"

"Ms. Helena's husband, Mr. Jackson."

"Oh, no. Poor Ms. Helena. I hope she's okay. I still remember the times when she babysat me. She makes the best peanut butter pecan cookies...mm...mm...good."

"Oh, don't worry about Ms. Helena. She's okay. Mr. Jackson was sick for a while. She expected it and is okay, especially since he made peace with God a few weeks ago. Mom said he'd really changed. She said that when he was strong enough, he'd beat Ms. Helena getting into church and sat right in the front row, daring anyone to take his favorite spot on that pew...right in the center on the left hand side of the church."

"Wow! You just never know," Sasha said as she stacked her books and placed them into her book bag. Walking over to the mantle, she began looking at the pictures that she'd already viewed thousands of times and became unusually quiet.

"What's wrong, Sasha?"

"Oh...nothing."

"Come on, Sasha-girl, I've known you long enough to know when something is not quite right with you. I can see it written all over that pretty little face of yours. What's up?"

Sasha always looked up to Jalena as a big sister and went to her for help in figuring things out that were vexing.

"Jalena, did you know that Mom is getting ready to move us down south?"

"Yes, she mentioned it, but I thought it was just all talk and that there would be no action placed behind it. I really didn't think she was seriously making such a life changing step, Sasha."

"But Jalena, it's not something that I want to do. This is home for me."

"Where down south is she planning to move?"

"Oh, some town called Powder Springs, Georgia."

"Really? Never heard of it before."

"Jalena, what do you think I should do? I don't want to leave my friends, and I'll really miss the times the two of us spend together. I just don't want to go!"

"Sasha, you really don't have a choice. When is all of this supposed to take place?"

"She's not sure yet...maybe in a couple of months. It may even be at the beginning of the new year. She's waiting for the paperwork at her job. It's a big promotion for her. Jalena, I know I should be happy for Mom. She says it involves a good pay raise, but I'm happy here."

"Sasha, you have to understand Aunt Jessie and what she's feeling. She wants a change in life. She wants better for you."

"I know...I know, J, but this is home for me. Even though there are some bad memories, there are more good ones and I've made a lot of friends that I would hate to leave. I don't want to go, but I also don't want Mom to leave here without me. She's the only mom who's really ever loved and cared for me."

There was panic in Sasha's words. "Why does she have to take me so far away from all of my friends and go way down there to a place no one has ever even heard of? They probably don't even have cell phone towers. How will I be able to stay in touch with all of my friends? What if it's hard for me to make new ones? Jalena, I'm scared!"

Sasha was ready to cry. This move was really affecting her and was more about her fear than anything else. Jalena tightly embraced Sasha as if she was trying to hug away the fear.

Jalena softly said, "Sasha, I know you will miss your friends. I, too, will miss the times you and I spend together, but I've learned something in the past few days...we have to learn to trust God and put away all fear. There may be many hidden reasons why this is happening, and that, only God knows. We can't always question the things that are happening. It's a part of life and if it's in the will of God, things will happen - regardless. There's nothing you, me or anyone else can do to change or stop destiny. Sasha, just think—it's not like we can't visit each other, right? Stop fretting, honey. It's going to be all right. It really will."

Sasha sniffled, grabbed a tissue from the holder and said, "Okay, J, but make me a promise?"

"What's that, Sasha?"

"Promise me that we'll talk to each other every day?"

"Sasha-girl, I can't promise you that. Maybe once a week? We'll see what happens. Okay?"

"Okay--I guess," she sadly said.

Jalena bumped shoulders with Sasha and said, "Now look at me. Look at me, Sasha."

She slowly turned her face to Jalena.

Smiling at Sasha, Jalena said, "Now listen, I want to see you smile. Come on, Sasha, you can do it. I want to see a great big smile on that face of yours."

A smile slowly replaced the sadness written on Sasha's face as she said, "Is there anymore of Auntie's coconut walnut cake leftover?"

Jalena chuckled and said, "There should be one little piece left just for you. Hopefully Jared hasn't gotten his big, grimy fingers in it and eaten it up! Come on, let's go check."

Sasha smiled as Jalena took her hand and they went into the kitchen. Jalena silently prayed for Sasha's peace and acceptance of the impending move.

Chapter 7

Jalena's brother, Jared has always thought of himself as the ultimate ladies' man...a prize catch for any young woman who was fortunate enough to capture his heart. Girls hung onto his every word and admired him for his looks. They also adored his pretty, full, brown lips. This was irritating to her. It always bothered Jalena when young girls stared at him. Walking in the mall or on the street, young girls and sometimes women would take a second look. He was a handsome young man — the spitting image of their dad in his younger days...5'9" with a muscular build, swarthy complexion, naturally curly, dark-brown, wavy hair and hazel colored eyes.

Jalena disliked Jared's choice of female companionship. They seemed to be the type of women that didn't quite fit the description of the "good girl" or classy type of women. Most times, she seemed to be quite a trouble maker...someone who had made her mark and left negative impacts on others in some way. This was the bottom line, it was hard for Jalena to deal with the fact that her baby brother was even old enough for these types of unhealthy pleasures.

She was very protective of Jared and always went toe-to-toe with any female he brought into her presence. In the past, she got into a lot of trouble with Jared, but felt she couldn't help herself in doing so. There were times when it seemed that Jared purposely made a game out of seeing Jalena's reaction when bringing girls around to meet her.

On this day, Jalena was sitting in the living room reading and listening to music on her IPad when Jared proudly walked into the living room with a new friend.

"Hey, Sis!" He kissed Jalena on the cheek and said, "Where's Mom?"

Side eyeing the girl, she said, "Mom went back over to visit Ms. Helena to see if she needs anything. Why?" Without taking a breath between words, she said, "Who is this? Aren't you going to properly introduce her?" She then paused, waiting for an answer.

Smirkingly he said, "Hey, give me a chance, will ya? This is my friend, Delia...Delia Morgan. Delia, this is my sister, Jalena."

Delia stretched out her hand to Jalena courteously, but Jalena declined.

She looks familiar, thought Jalena as she checked her out.

The rejection didn't stop Delia from greeting her warmly as she said, "Nice to meet you, Jalena."

Jalena was being rude. "Do I know you?" she asked. Jalena was trying to figure out where and when she had previously seen this new girl.

"Delia...Delia Morgan. Hey! Aren't you the girl that—" Jalena's questioning suddenly stopped. She figured out how she knew Delia, but decided to keep it to herself and said, "I've heard quite a bit about you."

Quickly responding, Delia said, "Oh yeah! It's all good. It's all good." Delia bowed her head in shame.

Jalena looked at her with narrow eyes and rudely said, "You think so?" She went back to her reading.

Jared was quiet. Jalena knew he was feeling the tension between her and Delia because he then tried to break the coldness as he stood and announced, "We're going to my room to do a little research."

Jalena snapped. "Are you crazy or something? How do you have the audacity to think that I would let something like that happen in this house while I'm sitting right here? Research...in your room? Jared, you must have lost your ever loving mind. Humph."

An argument ensued. "Jalena, for your information, Delia needs help with a project, and I promised to help her."

"Jared, you're out of high school and have been for a few years now. What are you now...a tutor offering your personal service to high school girls?" Jalena was angry.

"How old is she anyways? Did you think about that before you two got involved? I don't see any literature, no books, no papers. So explain your thinking to me. I'm confused!"

Jalena was on a rampage. "Exactly what will you be researching? Science exploration...physics, perhaps? You know as well as I do that if Mom were here, you wouldn't even try attempting such a ridiculous thing as taking a girl into your bedroom or even making the slight mention of that. Little brother, I'm laughing on the inside at you for even thinking that you can try and get away with something as ludicrous as that in this household. It's a total insult!"

She got to him. Jared was seething.

"Jalena!" he yelled. "What is your freakin' problem? For one thing, she's not in high school. Delia's my age. You know me better than that! I would never dishonor this house, mom and family like that! You're the only in this house that has the gall to do something so obnoxious as—"

When Jared realized what he was doing, he stopped mid sentence. He had just thrown the bitter past back up in Jalena's face. He could see the pain of past memories in his sister's face. Not wanting to dig up old skeletons in front of his guest, he calmly said to Jalena.

"We need to use my computer to pull up and print information...really."

Holding back tears, but in a much quieter and calm tone she said, "Mom would never approve of a girl in your room, and neither do I. So, Jared, no researching will happen in your bedroom while I'm here and Mom is away. If you need to do this project, you'll have to do it right here in this living room. Grab my laptop, get some paper and a pen to write down the info and get it done. That's all there is to it, Jared."

Jalena was so disappointed in Jared. How could he do that to her and why was he was trying to get away with taking a girl into his bedroom? Was this a repeat performance of what he'd done before? He had secrets too...secrets that only she, Jared and the girl who decided to abort his child. It was hidden from their mother. Jalena loved her mother too much to hurt her by revealing anything about the loss of a grandchild. Marinda would be devastated by such news. So Jalena's pride was now hurt, but she licked her wounds and dismissed her feelings and said, "You're so lucky Mom isn't here right now, she would —"

Apparently, Jared dismissed them too because before she could say another word, he yelled at the top of his lungs, "Since when did you get so self-freakin' righteous, Jalena? When?"

Delia stood mute the entire time...didn't say one word. Finally deciding she didn't want any more talk around her or involvement in the confusion and discussion, she shouted, "Stop! Stop all of this!"

Jalena and Jared were talking all over her as if she never existed. She was invisible as they demeaned each other.

Delia boldly said, "Jared...please...come on, let's get out of here. Let's just go. Come on. We'll go to my apartment." Looking at Jalena wide eyed, she continued, "Mom and Dad are out of town. We'll have the place all to ourselves. My Dad has a Mac computer, and we can research there without interruption."

Jalena was livid. Delia had figuratively slapped her in the face figuratively with those words. Before Jalena could clapback her disapproval, Jared turned away from her, took Delia by the hand and said, "Come on, Delia. Let's go."

"Wait!" yelled Jalena. They were out the door.

Jalena was angry but yet saddened by what had just taken place. Her brother brought up the bitter memories she didn't want to remember - memories that had greatly shaken the core of their family. She silently prayed. *Lord, help me! Take this offense and guilt away from me. The past is the past. I don't want it rehashing in my mind, so take it away from me now.* She read Psalm 91.

Chapter 8

For the past few days, Trisha, Jalena's best friend was consistently calling, but Jalena wouldn't answer. She didn't want to explain anything that had occurred within the past few days to Trisha. Besides, she knew the only reason Trisha was probably calling was to persuade Jalena to go out and party. It was something Jalena didn't want to do now that she had surrendered her life to God. Her experience at church changed her perspective on life. She needed and wanted to be better. Drinking and partying were the first things she wanted to learn living without.

Tired of the persistent ringing and vibration of her phone, she picked it up and answered.

"Hello, Trisha," she said, tiredly. Jalena tried keeping it cool with Trisha. She didn't want to lie her way out of this one. Besides, Trisha had a way of sensing if Jalena was being untruthful. Therefore, she had to be as honest as possible.

"Hey, Jalena. So what's up with you, kiddo? I tried calling earlier...a few times, in fact. I haven't seen or heard from you in a couple of days. What's going on? What's up with you?"

Jalena sighed and said, "Oh, I decided to stay in and catch up on some heavy reading. Mom and Jared are away. I just needed some time to think and get some things straight in my mind." That was as honest as Jalena wanted to get with her at that moment.

Trisha laughed and said, "J, girl, what are you talking about? What's going on with you? You don't sound good. What's happening?"

"Trisha, don't worry about it. I've got this. Believe me, I'm just fine."

Jalena thought she was in the safety zone as the conversation continued, but just before she tried to hang up, Trisha said, "Girl, you know what? You need to get out of that house...tonight. My cousins and I are clubbing tonight. Get dressed and we'll pick you up around ten. It'll be fun. Let's head over to the Black Maverick. We'll have a few drinks, a few laughs, get our dance on and watch the hotties. What you say, girl, what you say?"

This wasn't what Jalena wanted at all. Hesitation held her for a second and then she said, "I don't know, Trisha.

I'm kinda tired of that scene. Besides, this is a week night, and I've got the early shift in the morning."

Trisha had a hard time agreeing to anything once her mind was made up. It was usually her way or no way at all. She hated objections.

"Um...oh no...you're going with us. Something's up with you, J. Whatever it is, once you put on your little black dress and stiletto pumps, you'll get your groove on and be okay. Come on now. Get rid of the funk! Besides, we might run into Sage. You know how he feels about you. And you two need to cut this crazy BS out and get back together. That's all I'm saying. We'll pick you up at ten and I'm not taking no for an answer."

"But Trisha...Trisha?" The phone clicked. There was nothing but dead air and then a dial tone.

Chapter 9

She gave in and was ready when Trisha and her cousins, Tiffany and Khadijah, came to pick her up. Trisha was punctual and arrived at ten sharp. She blew the horn only once and then Jalena heard her outside yelling, "Come on, Jalena! You got one minute or I'm coming in for you."

The Black Maverick was a hot new club over the bridge on Belmont Avenue in the entertainment district. The club was one of the major attractions for the young, rambunctious crowd. Since its opening, police frequented on many occasions.

As Trisha made the turn around the bend, you could hear music blasting a block away and hear party goers shouting, "Ain't no party like an R&B party cause an R&B party don't stop." It was loud and poppin'.

Walking into the club, you could barely move through the outer vestibule. Some of the crowd made that area a dance floor because the main room was jammed packed. Finally making their way into the main area, Jalena was hit in the face by the sultry mix of heat and body-cologne scents.

The lights were turned down low and the room was lit by the soft glow of candles, which burned on oval-shaped white tables lining the walls along the long, rectangular hall. Red stage spotlights set the ambience for this packed venue as the band played for the excited crowd. On the floor, people danced as if hypnotized by the beat of the music, taking flight with each note played. Trisha, Jalena, Tiffany and Khadijah were surprised to find an empty table up front near the main dance floor.

Excitedly Trisha said, "All right, ladies. Here we go...a booth right in the middle of all the action. Looks like it was left here just for us."

She slid over into the seat, which was covered in red leather. Even though this was a relatively new place, the seating was worn. There were little holes showing the white cottony filling, threatening to make its way out as if to attack and ruin good clothing. As Jalena gingerly slid over into the booth, she thought, *I just got this black satin dress from the Donna Karan Collection on sale for half the price and I refuse to have one fiber pulled from it on these torn up, raggedy seats tonight. That just will not be the case.*

As she made her way in, Tiffany shouted, "Hurry up, Jalena! Why you movin' so slow?"

"Just wait! You're not rushing me, and I'm not messing up this new dress – so just cool it."

The music was blaring. People were dancing, laughing, shouting, "Hey…ho…hey…ho." They were having a great time. A local band, called Tribulation was on stage singing, "Move your body – shake that thang – movin' to the music – give it all you can bring." They were pretty good with great harmony and smooth blends.

Trisha, Khadijah and Tiffany moved to the power of the music, were popping fingers, laughing and singing. Jalena sat there listening, but did not allow the music to move her. Guilt was filling her heart as she sat there, watching her friends and the crowd around her. This was strange for her. She loved a good beat and could dance a roach off any floor. She was just no longer into this kind of entertainment.

Feelings had now changed. She was no longer the same. The music wasn't affecting her the way it normally did and Trisha noticed that she seemed to be out of sorts. Jalena wasn't acting the way she normally did.

Shouting over the loud music she said to Jalena, "Girl, what's up with you? This music is hot! What on earth has gotten into you? Let me order you a drink – Waiter!"

Jalena stopped her and said, "Trisha, no drink for me...not tonight. And...um...no more drinking for me from now on."

"Aw...come on, Jalena! Drink up. It's party time! Woop...woop!"

"Trisha, I don't want a drink! I'm here, what more do you want from me?"

You could hear the agitation in her voice. Jalena didn't want to be there in the first place. She never liked being forced to do something that she didn't want to do, but in this friendship, it had always been an issue. In the past, Jalena would always end up letting Trisha have her way in order to keep down confusion and arguments.

"Jalena, loosen up, girl! Come on, you're here now. You might as well enjoy it and have some fun. Shake it off! Oh, look, there's Sage!"

Jalena looked up and over in the direction Trisha pointed. She couldn't help but smile.

"He looks so good. The most handsome man I've ever seen," she said as he walked by.

Trisha thought seeing Sage would change Jalena's attitude and said, "There you go, J! That's what I'm talking about. Go over and talk with him. Get things straight.

You know you want him. This is perfect timing for the two of you lovebirds to get back together."

"Trisha, seeing him doesn't mean a thing and doesn't change a thing. I'm definitely not going to be the one who makes the first move – not tonight...not about to happen."

"You two are being so ridiculous. If I had a man that looks as hot as Sage, I'd be right there at his side before another sister snatches him up. Girl, you better open your eyes and take notice. I need a drink, and it's obvious you do, too – Waiter!!"

Jalena had finally had enough. She was ready to go. "Listen, Trisha, I don't need or want a drink. I'm out of here. I just can't hang anymore."

"We just got here, Sis. I don't know what it is or what's going on, but this is some crazy kind of mess, and I don't like it!"

The music was loud and it didn't matter that Jalena was now yelling. She was angry. "Trisha, this place is bad news. I'm just not comfortable with being here! I can't be here!"

"And why is that!" Trisha shouted back.

Jalena had tears in her eyes.

"What is it, Jalena? Why are you acting like this?"

Grabbing a napkin from the holder she said, "Something happened to me at church the other night.

"Church! You went to church?" Trisha was now raised her voice in anger.

In the past, they had numerous discussions about church that didn't end on a good note. Trisha had her opinion and Jalena had hers. There were heated arguments about the purpose of going to such an organization when you could get the same thing by watching television on any given Sunday morning. At least the preacher wouldn't be pocketing your money. Television was the best way in Trisha's eyes. She was adamant about that fact, and felt that only a bunch of hypocrites attended church. They were perpetrators of religious fraud.

There would always be a critical reminder from Jalena when the discussion got hot. "Listen, Trisha! Do not generalize! Don't put all Christians in the same category! My mother is not a hypocrite; she attends church regularly, so who are you talking about? Not my mother!"

Even though Jalena was not attending church at that time, she disagreed with Trisha and would always try to express her strong feelings in these regular debates. Jalena's mother had taught her better. So here she was, once again having to defend church attendance.

"Yes, I went to church with mom, and something I just cannot explain happened to me! Because of that experience, being here just doesn't feel right to me.

Something's not right. I'm in the wrong place. I can't do this anymore. It's just not for me."

"You're kidding, aren't you, Jalena? One hot and heavy service of you being hit by a 'supernatural something' has changed you just like that to the point of you not wanting to be here – in all this fun, laughter, dance and music? Sounds fishy to me! That's so whack, Jalena. You're just trippin'."

"Trippin'? You say I'm trippin'? Listen up, missy, that supernatural something, as you call it, is the Holy Spirit – something that you could use a little of right now. Please hear and understand me with clarity, Trisha. Things have changed in my life. I can't explain it right now and don't want to discuss it here in this place at this moment. At some point...somewhere else, we'll sit down and have a calm, adult-like conversation about all of this. I don't want to get into an argument over religion with you, Trisha. Until then, I'm out of here! I've got to go. If you see Sage again, please tell him I said hi. Okay? I love you, girl."

Jalena kissed Trisha on the cheek and walked away. She didn't want to argue with her friend; it didn't feel right, and she couldn't take it anymore.

As she struggled to get out of the booth past Trisha's cousins, Trisha had to have the last word, trying with a last-ditch effort to convince Jalena to stay.

"But, Jalena, you came with me!"

Jalena looked back at her and shouted, "Buses and taxis are running! I'll talk to you later. Love ya!"

Jalena walked away and called Jared. He picked her up. That was the last time she would ever see or hear Trisha's voice.

Approximately ten minutes after Jalena left the club, Trisha got caught up in another argument. It was over that raggedy booth in front, next to the dance floor. It seems to have belonged to someone else that had left the booth to get a drink. Trisha's refusal to give up that space led to a fight that ended in a shooting. Jalena's friend, Trisha Mirellas, was killed. Tiffany and Khadijah were on the dance floor, so they survived, but two other persons were trampled and killed that night in a race to exit the mayhem in the overcrowded building.

Chapter 10

"Peters, Simon and Jacobs. This is Jalena. May I help you? What? What did you say? What...No! Stop! Stop! You're wrong...No-o-o! Oh God! Oh God, no! Trishaaaa!"

A piercing scream escaped from Jalena's mouth and echoed throughout the office.

"Jalena, what's wrong? What happened? What is wrong with you?" Laurie ran to Jalena's side. Other colleagues looked up to see what all the commotion was about.

Jalena couldn't speak. A broken floodgate of burning tears ran down her face, as she dropped the phone and buried her face into Laurie's chest. She cried profusely. Jalena was just given the sullen news about her friend, Trisha. Sharina informed her of the tragedy. Word spread quickly on every local news channel about the incident. Trisha was killed at the club.

Once she was able to contain herself, Jalena called her mom. Marinda tried comforting Jalena over the phone and said that she'd been trying to leave the house to get to her before anyone told her the news, but the calls she was receiving all day long prevented Marinda from getting to Jalena in time. Friends and family members were concerned since they knew that Trisha and Jalena were best friends. Laurie got permission and gave her a ride home.

Walking into the house, Jalena could hear her mother praying, calling out Trisha's name and thanking God that He'd protected Jalena from the danger that unfolded. With tears flowing, Jalena rushed into the living room. She couldn't stop crying. In a state of shock and disbelief, she plopped down on the couch, feeling sick to her stomach. Jalena needed her mom and was glad she was there to comfort her. Before she could say one word, Marinda was by her side, embracing Jalena as if she were trying to take all of her pain and hurt away with a strong, loving touch.

"It's okay to cry...just let it all out...let it go...it will be alright, baby. It'll be alright."

"Mom...Trisha!"

"I know, I know. I'm so sorry, baby...I am so sorry."

All strength in Jalena's body was gone and was now replaced with immense sorrow and sadness. Her mother's hug was comforting. Jalena's best friend, Trisha was gone and at that moment, the feeling of losing her mind enveloped her. With her face buried into her mother's chest, a piercing, muffled scream left her weak body.

It hurt Marinda to hear her child in such painful grief. Struggling to hold back her own tears, she held Jalena close and rocked her until a calming peace swept over her body. Jalena was tired from the stress of all the drama and after crying for some time, she fell asleep in her mother's arms.

After a while, Jalena awakened. Marinda was still there and was softly singing as Jalena rested in her arms. When she noticed her daughter was awake, Marinda carefully removed the plastic wrap from the top of a glass of apple juice and handed it to her. Jalena took the small, crystal glass and drank until it was empty. Looking into her mother's eyes, Jalena asked, "Why...why, Mom? How could something so terrible as this happen?"

Pausing to gather her thoughts, Marinda sat back and looked up, as if searching for help in what she was about to say. The hesitation was short lived as she said, "Baby, I know you're grieving right now and you won't want to hear this, but I have to say it in order to answer your question."

She sighed and now looking at her daughter's tear stained eyes, she said, "We've all been gifted with choices in this world and are given many opportunities to decide how we're going to use those individual choices. Many times, we make decisions based on how we feel emotionally instead of looking to the Lord and asking His best advice first. We're given the power of choice to decide how we want to live: It's either in God's will or in our own carnal will. Trisha made a choice to live in her own will. She lived outside of the will of God and got swept up into a messed up, confused way of life. Baby, I know it hurts you to hear this, but you know I'm right. You once were out there in that world with and without Trisha and without God.

Remember the things the two of you got into? I know. Now it hurts to even look back on those ratchet days, right? But now, you've chosen God's way of doing things and many prayers have been answered and God's will for your life is now on the verge to be answered in abundance. I know it's hard for you to understand right now. The two of you were friends since grade school. You'll miss her. So cry if you must, but don't let that keep you from moving on and living your purpose-driven life."

Jalena rested in her mother's arms and began to feel a peacefulness that could only be explained as God's peace that surpasses all understanding. His presence was there as she listened to her mom speak these words of wisdom with clarity. Jalena felt strengthened and said, "I was there...right there, and as soon as I left--that could have been me, Mommy...it could have been me. I was sitting there right next to her and I left her...I left my friend...I left her there and then this happened."

"Child, I just thank my God that He was there with you and got you up and out of that place at the right time. His grace and mercy never fail to amaze me. Now listen, don't you get caught up in a guilt trip, trying to figure out why. Just thank God that you are here, in the land of the living, and that He wrapped you in His loving arms to get you out of harm's way. We'll pray for the lives of your friends that are still out there in the world, caught up in a confused and messed up way of life. Let's not forget Trisha's mom; she must be so torn up right now. One day, God will help all of us to understand this clearly, but in His own time. All we can do for now is pray."

"But it just doesn't make any sense, Mom...it just doesn't."

"Not everything in this life will ever make sense to anyone of us, Jalena. Despite that, we have to wait on God and stand on our faith. We have to keep our focus on what God has for us to do and let Him lead the way. No matter what, God is to be glorified. Let's pray."

Sitting on the couch, they grasped each other's hands and began to pray. After prayer, Jalena went to her bedroom and cried herself to sleep, hoping that this bad dream would soon be over. She slept and awakened the next day.

Chapter 11

Ding Dong.

"Who is it?"

A new day had dawned, and Jalena was settled in her mind that her friend was gone. Sadness filled her heart, but she knew it wouldn't make any sense to stay in this state of grief. If she did, it would most likely lead to severe depression—a place she had been on more than one occasion. It was a place that, in the past, caused her to go into drinking frenzies, drug-crazed nights and binge-eating episodes. She didn't want to open the door to past demons and make room for that to happen again. Therefore, she prepared to attend the funeral service and made up her mind to honor Trisha's memory by choosing to live on purpose through all of the great times they spent together.

Ding Dong.

"Who is it?"

"Sage!"

"Sage?"

Genuine excitement filled her heart just knowing that on the other side of the door, he stood there...wanting to see her. Jalena ran to the wall mirror to check herself out and then even took a second look into a smaller framed mirror sitting on top of the coffee table. She slowly walked to the door, hesitating before placing her hand on the gold doorknob; she didn't want to seem too anxious to Sage about his visit. Taking a long, deep breath, she could feel her heart pumping fast as she finally opened the door and gave way to his entrance.

She calmly said, "Hi, Sage. What are you doing here?" Deep within, Jalena was feeling an overwhelming joy and felt the fluttering of her heart as she looked into the eyes of her beautiful, copper skinned Adonis with dark gray eyes and brush-cut wavy hair. This relationship had caused her to be the envy of some of her friends and girls who were not even acquainted with Jalena. At one point, she even thought Trisha was trying to hit on Sage when she wasn't around. Trisha denied it and convinced Jalena otherwise.

A petty argument caused their mutual decision to take a break from each other. In Jalena's heart, she always hoped that the breakup would be short lived.

"Can I come in?" he softly said.

Fully opening the door, Jalena let Sage in. "I saw you at the club with Trisha...I had to make sure you were okay and couldn't rest until I did."

Sage was talking fast and seemed to be nervous as he spoke. "Jalena, I feel your pain. Are you...okay? I mean...the two of you were so close, growing up together...the hurt has to be intense. I can't even begin to know or even imagine how you must be feeling right now...I needed to check on you, Jalena."

With tear filled eyes, she said, "Yes, it hurts, but I'm okay...I guess. I've been trying to keep my mind on other things and only remember the times that make me smile about our relationship. I'm trying, but it's been hard. I have to make it work; I can't let it take me back to where I've been in the past. I've come too far to let the grief take control of my mind."

Jalena walked away from him. She didn't want to lose control and burst into tears.

"Sage, what happened? Do you know? Did you see anything? You were there. How could something like this happen?"

"I'm not sure, baby. I was there, but I only stopped in for a short time to drop off money to the manager for a gig I was planning to have there and left when I saw you leaving. All I know is what I heard."

"What did you hear?"

"Are you sure you want to hear this, Jalena?'

"Yes, I need to...really need to."

Sage took a seat on the sofa and said, "Well, Trisha got into an argument over the table where they were seated. That table was reserved for Black Storm."

"Black Storm, the drug dealer?"

"Yes. In the middle of that argument, some other guys came in, and another heated argument started with Storm over some money. He dismissed them and after dancing with his girl he returned to his table and asked Trisha to remove herself. She refused to give in and just sat there. Trisha started a full blown argument with his girl, talking about how she didn't see a nameplate engraved on that table with his name and she wasn't moving."

The tears started flowing down Jalena's face as she said. "Oh, Trisha...why do you always have to get in the last word? Didn't she know who he was?"

Shaking his head, Sage said, "Apparently not. That's when those guys came over to Black Storm's table and continued demanding their money, brought out a gun and pulled the trigger. A missed shot caught Trisha in the temple. All hell broke loose with everyone trying to get out of the way. They haven't caught the shooter yet, but they've a really good description. Black Storm was down at the Livingston Precinct all night being questioned. It's all over the news."

"Sage, I still can't believe this! She's gone! I was praying that all of this was a nightmare that I'd somehow awaken from."

Jalena sat next to Sage and he embraced her. He gently said, "Babe, you know, things like this really open your eyes...I mean...we were there and could have easily been shot and killed. J, you were sitting at that table with her. It could've been you if you stayed there, sitting with Trisha. I don't know what I'd have done if it had been you."

As Sage was talking about losing Jalena, tears welled up in his eyes. She took his hand, as they sat there in total grief. Jalena wiped the tears from his eyes and said, "Sage, I feel the same way. I lost Trisha and wouldn't have wanted to lose you, too. That's a pain I'd never want to feel."

Jalena thought about what might have been and shed tears without shame.

Sage then asked her, "What made you leave? I asked Trisha and she just shook her head saying, 'I don't know...must be her time of the month.'"

"What! She actually said that! Wow!"

"Yes, she did, but she also said she was worried about you and told me what was said about church. She seemed agitated about that. I went outside looking for you, but you were gone. What happened to make you leave? Don't get me wrong, I thank God you did."

"Sage, I had to leave. I left because I was not feeling comfortable there. Something inside of me wasn't settling right. Today I know that it had to be God who filled me with that discomfort and made me leave! He got me out of harm's way. He knew what was about to go down."

Overwhelmed, Jalena cried uncontrollably. A feeling of relief, but also guilt filled her heart. "I'm grateful for His protection, but at the same time, I'm feeling a bit of guilt because I didn't try to talk Trisha into leaving with me...oh my poor Trisha!"

Sage hated seeing Jalena like this, so he held her, trying his best to give comfort.

"J, please don't cry like this and don't go placing any blame on yourself. It must have been her time."

Jalena quickly pulled away from Sage. His words offended her. "What did he say? It must have been her time?"

Jalena was feeling the pain and hurt of losing her friend and thought these were hateful words coming from him.

"How can you say such a thing? It must have been her time?"

"Jalena, I'm so sorry, baby...I'm sorry...I know it hurts; the two of you were best buddies. I apologize!"

Looking at him thoughtfully, she then laid her head on his chest. She knew he was not trying to be offensive - he was only trying to help her. Sage took a handkerchief from his pocket and gave it to Jalena.

Smiling through her tears, she said, "Is this clean? I mean, there aren't any buggers on it...right?"

Sage smiled back and said, "Really?"

Jalena wiped away her tears and said, "You're right. Maybe it was her time."

They sat silently for a moment.

Sage kissed her forehead and said, "I'm here for you, and I promise to help you get through this terrible pain. Just tell me what you need. I want to help...I'm not going to ever leave you again; I promise. I've really missed you so much."

"I've missed you too, Sage...missed you so much."

"Let me tell you this, J. My love for you has never diminished, and I'm so sorry for everything I've done to hurt you. I was just going through some of my own personal mess. Those petty arguments we had never had any effect on the love I feel for you. I apologize for over-reacting. I was going through some past emotional issues that had my head all messed up. I'm back and want to help you in any way that I possibly can. Will you please just let me do that?"

Jalena could never refuse this man who was the love of her life. Their love was always there, even in the breakup. When their eyes met, passion was stirring. There was no resistance as their lips met and kissed passionately. They were soon lost in each other's arms. Sage was back, the kindling was stirred and was now burning in their hearts as they reunited as one.

Chapter 12

Next to the death of Jalena's dad's, the few days following Trisha's demise were the hardest and longest days of her life.

Trisha's mom called and made a special request saying, "Jalena, you and Trisha were like sisters and had such a great bond. I'd like for you to sit with the family at the service. Trisha would've wanted that."

There was no way she could refuse. Trisha was her sister...her friend. Jalena was happy to fulfill the request.

The funeral service turned out to be a beautiful tribute. The community packed a chapel on the cemetery grounds. There was singing, liturgical dancing and words from Trisha's friends, of which Jalena was a part. Standing behind the mahogany pulpit, the words she wanted to express were stuck in the back of her throat as burning tears began to flow. Sage quickly made his way to her as a show of support and grabbed her quaking hand. She wanted to be strong when she made her speech, but this was hard. Her best friend was lying there in a pink, silver trimmed casket in front of her. How would she say what she wanted to say without feeling this heavy weight of pain piercing her heart?

Jalena stood there for a moment. People in the congregation shouted words of encouragement.

"That's alright, baby...cry if you want! Let it out! It's okay to cry!"

Sage embraced Jalena and took a handkerchief from his pocket and wiped away her tears. Resting her head upon his shoulder, she suddenly felt as if Trisha's spirit was next to her--watching, pushing and telling her, "Girl, just go ahead and say what you gotta say. Speak up and be bold about it; stop being a wimp."

Jalena thought about Trisha's boldness and how if it were the other way around, Trisha would have no problem in speaking out for Jalena. So she took in a deep breath, stood tall and spoke up. She shared her heart and love for her sister by telling them how they met and the battle that ensued with water paint on their first day of school. It made people laugh; it brought smiles to their faces. She knew in her heart that it was what Trisha would've wanted. Jalena was glad that she finally had enough strength and courage to perform the task with Sage by her side and Trisha's spirit pushing her on.

Community leaders stood and encouraged people to come together to prevent this type of violence from happening again. Aaron Tenningham, a local city politician said, "We can no longer tolerate this kind of behavior. The lives of our young citizens are at risk, and we should all be concerned and ready to war for their lives. If we have to close it down, then people, let's close it. Let's do it! They shall live and not die!" People stood, shouting, "Amen! Hallelujah! Say it! Preach the word, sir!" There was an air of urgency and commitment to change that emanated from those in attendance.

The service ended with a moving eulogy by Pastor Gregory Boyd. He closed his message by saying, "What will you do today? Are you ready to change and live a destiny-filled, fruitful life?" It was strange to see an altar call given at a funeral, but a few people made their way to the altar to give their lives to the Lord. This was not something Trisha would've done or agreed to, but despite that fact, it was good to see it take place.

Tahlia closed the service with a beautiful solo. As she sang the lyrics, "Though you may cry and feel like giving up, you just hold on...hold on...God is with you...He'll see you through," the tears began to flow. Crying uncontrollably, Trisha's mom ran up to the closed casket and laid her head upon it, embracing it as if trying to hold onto Trisha. It was heartbreaking to see her pain. Jalena couldn't bare it any longer and rushed out into the vestibule. Sage and her mom followed giving Jalena comfort while the last viewing took place. Jalena couldn't bear going to the gravesite; they left the chapel and went home. For Jalena, it was over. Her friend was gone.

Trisha never liked talking about the existence of God in her life and shunned going to church. On more than one occasion, she said, "When I get myself together, I'll go to church. I just don't want to be sitting up in any-body's church perpetrating Christianity, being something that I'm not. I have to change first." She knew that she wasn't the best person but felt she wasn't the worst, and disliked hypocritical Christians. Jalena felt sad that Trisha never got to experience what she was now feeling in her heart since she made the decision to surrender to the will of God.

Jalena was glad the ceremony was over. She knew things would never be the same without Trisha and hungered for some kind of happiness to take place that would move her heart away from sadness and give some semblance of peace. For right now, being home gave her what she needed. Marinda was out shopping, and Jared was at work.

Looking into the hallway closet, she got down on her knees and carefully pulled out a large, red-velvet box that her mom was very protective of. It was a memory box. Marinda stored pictures of every important moment from the time that Jared and Jalena were born. There are hundreds of mementos in that box.

On the day she found out that she was pregnant with Jalena, her first child, she hand decorated the box for posterity. Marinda told Jalena how she took it with her to the hospital and even brought it into the delivery room.

She wanted a picture of her newborn baby right from the womb and told her husband, "James, you make sure you get a picture of our baby as soon as she breathes air, but make sure they first get all that gunk off of her."

He did as she said and took the picture, placing it right into the box. Never skipping a beat, he kept on clicking away on his camera. He even took pictures of Marinda in the wheel chair on the day they left the hospital.

She made sure that there was a piece of history portraying every part of their lives through pictures, notes and memorabilia. Marinda even kept baby teeth in a little plastic bag in the box. She also kept her children's first pair of baby shoes and hung their christening outfits in a heavy plastic bag stuck in the back of the closet.

Digging through the unorganized mess, Jalena pulled out photos of her and Trisha. She felt that these memories would keep her sane and help to move her past the grief she was feeling. There was a picture of the two of them on their first day at school with paint all over their faces and clothes. She remembered on that day how Mrs. Meyers sat them in a corner, and told them, "Say cheese, I want your moms to have a copy of this picture. What a mess."

Jalena wondered where Matthew Dillion was today. "Where's he at and what's he up to," she said aloud.

As she perused more and more pictures, she was filled with smiles and, at times, even laughter as she waded through the pictures and thought about their journey together. Calming thoughts filled her mind.

We've really changed. Trisha was always the clever clown of the crew. She always had the punch line for any given situation, even as a child. She was a true friend. If no one else had your back, you could always count on Trisha to be the one who would jump to the front of the crowd, making sure you were okay. She took over when you were falling and couldn't get up.

There was one day in middle school when this boy named Michael Calutti tried to jump bad with me. I had it under control, but as soon as Trisha came on the scene, she jumped right in his face and said, "Michael Calutti, get your fat bootee away from here and leave my sister alone." He stood there, trying to be bold and staring her down, like he was so big and bad; he finally gave in and walked away. He never bothered me again. *What is life going to be like without you, my friend?* Her eyes began to burn with tears as she gazed at the photos.

Who will go shopping with me and scream with me during scary movies? We'd made plans that one day I would be your Maid of Honor and you'd be mine. You were supposed to be the godmother of my children, too!

Tears streamed down Jalena's face as the memories bombarded her mind, but a smile returned as she thought about the day that they became mature women. *It was just like clockwork. That was something else! I was so upset when I realized what was happening. My cramps were unbearable. I wasn't prepared for any of it - but you, my friend, were. You had everything both of us needed right there in your purse and taught me how to use them. I'm truly going to miss you so much. I love you, Trisha Mirellas. Love you so much, girl.*

Chapter 13

J alena was up early the next morning. Trying to get back into a regular prayer and Bible study routine was hard - but with determination, she made every effort. She had to make this step an important part of her life; it helped to strengthen and take her mind away from all the drama that happened during the last few weeks. She sat surrounded by various reference materials taken from her mom's bookshelf.

"I smell coffee!" Marinda shouted as she reached the bottom of the stairs. "And it smells so good!"

Jalena smiled proudly. She had already set up the dining room table and prepared a tasty breakfast of scrambled eggs, grits, toast with strawberry jam and bacon that was cooked just the way her mom liked it: hard and crispy but not burned to a crisp.

Her boss, Mr. Peters had given her the next few days off, and she wanted to use the days for some stress-free living. It felt good to have this little time of freedom.

"Everything looks so yummy," Marinda said as she went into the kitchen and eyed the food that Jalena had placed in the warming tray. "I'm going to enjoy every last bite. Where's Jared?"

"I'm here, right here," he said as he came rushing down the stairs, almost tripping on the rug when he hit the last step.

"Be careful, Jared. The food's not going anywhere. I cooked enough for everyone," said Jalena.

In a preachy voice he then said, "The delectable delicious smell of the bacon was my alarm clock early this morning. Can I get an amen?" Laughing, Jalena and Marinda said "Amen", in unison.

Sitting at the mahogany table, they joined hands and Marinda blessed the food. She thanked God for the fellowship and presence of her children. This little gesture from God was making her day complete before it even began.

"Do you have any plans for today, Mom?" Jalena asked as she spread strawberry jam on her toast.

"Yes, I do," she said with excitement. "I'm going to meet Deaconess Massey and Sister Shalon at the church thrift shop. We're going to volunteer for a few hours today and then have lunch. We've been trying to put items in order by category, color and size to make everything easier for people when they come into the shop. I've come across some really nice things people have brought in. I even picked up a sweater in the store yesterday that's nice and warm."

"Sounds great, Mom," said Jared after sipping his coffee.

Smiling at her son, she then said, "You two should come in and take a look; you may find something nice you weren't expecting to see. I'm telling you, we've got some name-brand styles that have come in within the last few days. The mayor's wife even dropped off a few suits that are still in the back room and haven't been marked or placed on racks yet."

"Really, Mom. Really," said Jalena as she bit into her toast. "I cannot go in there and pick up some second-hand stuff that has already been worn, even if it's from the mayor's wife. I just can't do it. It wouldn't feel or look right. Besides, I've had my eye on this beautiful, cranberry-red maxi cardigan at Harborplace Mall. I'm waiting to try it on again and will probably make a purchase this weekend. I'm hoping the price will drop just a wee bit more before making my move on it."

With a hint of disappointment, Marinda said, "Well, alright. I'm just trying to help you save some money. I'm telling you, there are some nice things in the shop, and there are even some cardigans that probably look just like the one you saw at the mall. You need to go in and check it out."

"Sorry, Mom, I just don't think so. Can't do it."

"Well, baby girl, one day you'll want to save a little piece of money and will remember this conversation, especially when you start making wedding plans."

"Wedding plans? Who said anything about getting married? I might just like the idea of being single for the rest of my life."

Marinda knew her daughter was joking and totally ignored the comment. This was not the first time this topic came up. While eating a bowl of popcorn and watching a movie, there were plenty of nighttime conversations on the subject of marriage and children.

Jared listened intently as he enjoyed his meal. Scraping the grits off his plate he said, "Hmm..."

Looking over at her brother, Jalena said, "So what does that mean? Hmm..., Jared Mathesin?"

"Well, Sis, for one thing, I know you've been hanging with Sage a lot lately. There's no way on God's green planet that Sage is going to let you get away this time without putting a ring on your boney, little finger."

"Oh, you think?"

"No, I know," he said confidently.

Marinda sat there with a smirk on her face and seemed to be enjoying every moment of their little conversation and said, "I for one love Sage. He is the perfect man for you. I love the thought of one day having a bona fide doctor in the family. That man is trying to make something happen in his life, and I'm so proud of him. You don't find too many young men out there today having a dream, vision and goal for life and taking measures to step right into that arena of pursuit, following dreams. It's very rare."

That comment started a fire in Jared and he said, "Well, I guess it doesn't make me look too good, does it? Where does that leave me, Mom?"

Surprised by his comment, she looked into his eyes and said, "Jared, I've always been proud of you. You've been such a blessing to me. You stepped into manhood quickly to take care of this family, and I'm so grateful to God for you. Just know that He has many blessings in store for your life. I love you so much, Jared. I really don't know what I would've done without you taking over the way you have."

"Awww," said Jalena, picking up a napkin and faking tears.

"Why'd you do that, Jalena? You always got something negative to say. You're just jealous that I'm the favorite child," he said, eating his last bit of toast.

Jalena seemed a bit disconcerted and said, "What did I say? You know what? I'm going to let you get away with that one. You're right, I'm wrong. I'm in too good of a place mentally right now, and I don't want to get into it with you, little brother. Not right now, not today. Love you, Bro."

Quickly standing up and gathering his empty plate and silverware, Jared said, "Well, it's the truth, so just handle it, Jalena - just handle it!"

Marinda broke into the argument and said, "All right, you two! I love you both equally, and you're important to me. Let's not end this lovely breakfast on a sour note. Okay?"

"Oh...Okay, Mom. Sorry, Jalena. Love you, Sis!"

Jalena sighed and said, "No...I'm really sorry for making light of what Mom said to you. She's right, Jared. I thank you for all you've done for this family. I love you. You're the man!"

Everyone was smiling again. Marinda was especially happy and said, "Now you two clean up this mess while I get ready and get out of here. Thank you for the delicious meal, baby girl."

"You're welcome."

"Yeah, thanks, J." He kissed her on the cheek.

Jalena couldn't help but smile even harder. She was filled with pride knowing that even though sadness was still in her heart, she could make it through the day if she put her mind to it. Closing the door on sadness and ejecting it from her feelings and thoughts was a hard decision, but was made in order to live with purpose and not let it kill or destroy her joy.

Chapter 14

L ater in the day, Sage picked Jalena up and took her to lunch. Before he pulled off, he seemed a little nervous and said, "Jalena, I have to make a stop on our way to the restaurant."

"Really, where?"

"The club. The Black Maverick," he said pensively.

With his response, Jalena's face dropped. Sage knew that it was a big mistake to include her in this errand, but he had no other recourse.

"J, I'm sorry but with the fallout and all the bad publicity, I need to cancel and get a refund on the graduation gig that I scheduled to have there. Everything has left a sour taste in my mouth, but most important of all, I don't want to place you in a position of returning there. I tried earlier this week to get in contact with management and even this morning, but this was the only time he'd be available."

Jalena vowed to herself that she'd never, ever go back to that place and was glad Sage was sensitive to her feelings.

Hunching her shoulders, she softly said, "I'll be okay."

Sage knew it would be stressful and said, "It really bothers me having to do this, but if I don't go today, I may lose my money. There's a lot of talk on the streets about closing it down. The manager is fighting it, but he's losing ground. I'm afraid if they decide to close it down, I'll lose my money."

Sighing, he said, "Babe, I'm not asking you to go in with me, but are you sure you're able to handle sitting in the car and waiting? If you think it will cause bad memories to resurface, I'll go and come back and get you."

"No, Sage, I'll be okay – really, I will."

They drove off. Getting to the club, Sage went inside and Jalena waited silently, prayed asking God to heal her heart and calm the discomfort she felt. Even though she'd assured Sage that all was well, nervousness overcame her and did not leave until she saw him coming out of the building and walking towards the car.

Putting his face on the glass outside and looking in at her, he smiled. As soon as he got into the car, his smile turned into concern as he asked, "Are you all right, babe? I tried getting back as quickly as possible, but the manager gave me a lot of papers to sign just to get the refund. He had a stinky attitude...so unnecessary, if you ask me."

Jalena grabbed and hugged him and said, "I'm all right now that you're here with me." All discomfort subsided, and she was able to relax as they drove away from the building and were now on their way to the restaurant.

"Were you able to get all of your money back? I know sometimes establishments will try keeping a small percentage for cancelled booking fees."

"He tried to keep 15% of my money. Can you believe that? But, I reminded him that Barry Porterfield, the building inspector, is my uncle and if he didn't want me to make mention of him in any future conversations, that he'd better return every penny of what I gave him."

"Sage, you really threatened him like that?"

"I certainly did! You should have seen him signing that receipt and handing over my money just to get me out of that joint."

"I didn't know Mr. Porterfield was your uncle? Wait a minute. He's not your uncle...is he?"

"Well, kind of. He dated my Aunt Cora a few times and even came to the house for dinner on more than one occasion. I think he had a thing for her, but she wasn't that into him."

"Sage, that doesn't make him your uncle."

"He doesn't have to know that bit of information." They laughed at Sages antic.

"Now, let's go get some grub," he said as he drove away.

Finally making it to their destination, Sage pulled into the parking lot. Shutting off the car, he promptly jumped out and ran around to the other side of the car and opened the door for Jalena. He then took her by the hand, helped her from the car and closed the door gently behind Jalena. He always treated her like a princess no matter where they were. Even in high school, he carried her books, walked her to the classroom and opened doors, even if it made him a little late for his class. Sage was always the perfect gentleman.

Entering into the restaurant, the hostess greeted them. Dressed in a navy blue dress with a white collar, she addressed them saying, "Hello and welcome to Lady-Treana Cafe! Would you like a booth or a table?"

Sage spoke first and said, "We'd like a booth, please." She escorted them to a quiet corner in the back of the restaurant.

"Thank you, Miss, this is good," Sage said as she laid menus on the table and walked away.

Where they were seated was nice and cozy with the sunlight shining brightly through a large bay window. Beautiful yellow tulips were artistically formed on mosaic glass tiles on the lower half of the framed window, which sat in front of the small booth.

Sage perused the menu. "I'm so hungry – didn't get to eat breakfast this morning so I'm going to have breakfast for lunch. J, are you ready to order?"

"I'm ready to eat right now and already know what I want."

The waitress returned with a pitcher of fruit infused water and poured some into their glasses.

"Are you ready to place your orders?" she asked.

Without hesitation, Sage said, "Yes, we are. Jalena, go ahead; you order first."

Handing the menu back to the waitress, she said, "I'm going to have a turkey, pepper, onion and spinach quiche with a glass of sweet tea, please."

"What kind of toast would you like with that?"

"Hmm...Rye, please."

"Okay - and you, sir? What would you like to order?"

"I'll have some buttermilk pancakes, ham, grits and scrambled eggs," he said, smiling at the waitress.

"Sage, honey, I thought you were trying to watch your waistline and trim down your abs," chuckled Jalena.

"I am. I am, just not today," he said laughing.

The waitress took his menu and said, "Thank you! It will be up shortly."

As they waited for their order, Sage began reminiscing about the first time they met.

"I remember the very first time I saw you, J. Do you remember? It was at the old Woolworth's on Main Street. You were there with your godmother. I think you called her Cousin Mable - right?"

"Yes...Mable Bowman," said Jalena as she picked up her glass and took a sip of water.

"You were Easter shopping. It's funny how she and my Aunt Cora were good friends. They stood there for what seemed like hours, just talking and catching up. Neither one of us said a word; we just stood there staring at each other. You had a red pop in your mouth, just staring me down with your big brown eyes. You must have been what, 10 years old?"

"Yes, 10 and you were 14. I remember because Cousin Mable asked you your name and how old you were. You hesitated at first like you were shy or something and I was upset because I wanted some white, lace gloves to wear with my new Easter outfit and she couldn't find a pair anywhere in the store. I wanted that conversation to end quickly so that we could leave and get my gloves somewhere else. I thought you were cute, though. I was purposely trying to stare you down, but you never retreated. You never blinked your eyes."

"Jalena, I knew that's what you were doing; I couldn't let you win. When you left, I was hoping that one day we would meet again--and look at this--here we are today, together...prophecy. I'm so glad we ended up in the same high school. Wow!"

At that moment the waitress returned with their food, setting it on the table. Once it was all in place, Sage grabbed hold of Jalena's hands and blessed the food. While he was praying, Jalena looked up at him with admiration. She couldn't help but watch him, thanking God for blessing her with his friendship and love. She knew within her heart that one day her future with him would become a beautiful reality. Her life would be complete with this man who was sitting before her.

Chapter 15

"**G**oodnight, Mom, I love you!"

"Goodnight, Jalena, love you more!"

"Hey, ladies, what about me? Do you love me?"

"Jared, you're home!"

"Yes, Mom. Just got in. It's been a long day. Does anyone have any love for me? Do you love me?"

"Not much, brother dear."

"Wow, Jalena, you really know how to hurt a fella."

"Jared, you know I love you! You are my best brother, ever!"

"Your one and only brother, Jalena"

"Yes, you are, and I do love you, Jared!"

"Thanks, J. Love you, too!"

Mom chimed in on the jibber jabber and said, "I love you too, Jared. More than words can say, and there's a plate of spaghetti and meatballs in the fridge for you. Just stick it in the microwave for a few minutes—not for too long, though. Don't overcook it."

"Thanks, Mom. I love you too! Goodnight, ladies!"

In unison, Marinda and Jalena said, "Goodnight, Jared!"

Although she had never said it in so many words to him, Jalena was proud of her little brother. Even with his penchant for women and thinking of himself as the ultimate ladies man, he always made sure that the family came first. He took care of business. When their father died, Jared stepped in place and became the man of the house. Since that time, he managed everything with much grace and pride. His dad taught him well.

It was hard for Jared those first few days after the burial. He was still in high school. Trying to handle his school work along with working as an assistant mechanic at the local Shell gas station was his saving grace in being able to take care of household matters. Graduation could not come soon enough. Jalena held back tears as he crossed the stage with an honor degree in his hand and a big, cheesy smile on his face as he looked in their direction. Marinda sat there crying like a baby. As hard as she tried, Jalena finally let her tears go, wishing that their father was here to see his son graduating from school and taking the next big step into real manhood.

Unfortunately, Jared's dreams of serving in the United States Navy ended because of his commitment in not wanting to leave them alone. Even though his mom was working a part-time job to make ends meet, it made no difference to Jared. His family came first and no matter how much Marinda tried talking him into it, he wasn't hearing her. So he worked hard every day to prove that he was man enough to handle family business.

Proudly he said to Jalena, "My goal is to make sure we won't have to depend solely on yours or Mom's income to take care of this family. Besides, what would Daddy do?" That became his mantra as he kept moving forward every day to stay on top of family finances. He most certainly was the man of the house. Love was his motivation.

"Get some good rest tonight, Jared, I love you!"

"I'll try, J. Love you, too! Good night."

"Goodnight, Jared."

As Jared made his way into the kitchen, he sat down at the table, holding his head and rubbing his temples, and thought, *I wish this headache would just go away! I never thought this day would ever end...feeling so sick...this has to be the flu.*

Taking the food from the refrigerator, and looking at it he thought, *I'm not sure if I'm even able to eat this...my throat is burning hot. I'll try to at least eat a little of it and then I really need to go to bed. I've been so tired lately... I can't be getting sick...got too much to take care of.*

Chapter 16

J alena laid in bed and thought about the day she spent
with Sage.

*Whew...can't stop yawning. Spending the day with
Sage really wore me out. It's been a long day. Lunch at
Lady Treana's, went to the movies, visited Sage's friend at the
VA hospital and then my favorite thing of all - we went to
Harborplace, for a nice late dinner at The Brewing Factory. I
even got to see if my cardigan was still there. Thank God, it's
there and even down a few dollars. Being with Sage and having
this peace of mind feels real good. I think I'll finally be able to
get some good, restful sleep tonight. Now come on, blanket,
make me feel good, warm and cozy. Mmm...Sage. Ooh...let me
make a journal entry before I go to sleep.*

September 22 – *Sage, you alone could possibly one day
become my husband and the father of our children. I love you*

so much, and I know that Mom and the rest of the family already adore you because you are a man of worth - not monetarily, but because you are a man who has dreams, visions and goals for your life. I pray that I'm the one to share in those dreams. I am so proud of you. Look at you! You're in the last months of medical college and will soon be starting your residency program. Your dream of one day becoming a pediatrician will be here before you know it. Mom's constantly reminding me that you're a good catch (as if I didn't already know it). I just don't want to move too quickly into any kind of intimate relationship while you're still pursuing your degree. Besides, marriage has to come first before I can ever even think of giving myself to any man. I can't help smiling just knowing that man may one day be you, Sage, and I'm looking forward to it. Love you!

It was time to sleep. Jalena's eyelids were getting heavy.

With the blanket wrapped tightly around her body, she was delighted and said, "Mmm...blanket feels so good."

She then prayed and quietly said, "Dear God, you know I've been away for a while; I've been hitting and missing and just saying a quick prayer here and there. Mom used to make us pray as children, but when we got old enough and bold enough we stopped praying and started doing our own thing. I'm sorry for all I've done and how I've ignored You. I know You're a forgiving

God, and I ask You to forgive and take me back. I want to know You and be all that You want me to be. I beg Your pardon and now I present my life to You, acknowledging that You are my Lord and King. Help me to grow up in You. I'll follow hard after You and bless Your name. Thank You, Lord God, in Jesus' name. Amen!"

Wearied from her day, sleep came fast as her eyelids drooped and closed. Falling into deep sleep, her spirit drifted into a beautiful, bright blue place – a place filled with large, white, airy, cumulus clouds. At first she was alone, but then she heard a fluttering sound. She was suddenly surrounded by a host of angels as they danced on clouds above her. Jalena was in heaven. The angels moved to a melody sung by heavenly voices with the purest of harmonies. Accompanied by the tones of flutes, harps and various chimes, the voices rang throughout the air.

The angels floated through the air like feathers blowing in the wind as they fluttered their gold trimmed wings. One of them reached out, took Jalena by the hand and compelled her to dance. She was dressed in a pure white, long flowing, princess-cut gown with a red ribbon around her waist that wafted in the breath of the wind as she floated through the air like one of the angels who lifted her high. Suddenly, the host surrounded her and a powerful sounding voice called out her name. The crystal-clear voice startled Jalena, and an angel who stood above the rest calmed her as he said, "Fear not, Jalena. It is He, the King of Kings and Lord of Lords. It is God!"

Jalena then saw a bright, white light and felt the touch of the wind as it enveloped her entire being. She felt a sweet, peaceful presence. There was the scent of rose petals as He gently took her by both hands, moved slowly with the breeze and they danced among the angels. As they floated through the air, the sweet scent surrounded them as the once powerful voice transitioned to a still, small voice and whispered into her ears. He told her things that were meant exclusively for Jalena as they danced among the clouds.

"My child, I have watched you from a distance. From the time you were in your mother's womb, I had plans for you but you took a detour from the path which had been set specifically for you. The pace of what I had intended for you was delayed, but it now pleases me that you have returned your heart and soul to me. We can now continue on this journey I have planned for you. There will be many stumbling blocks that will try delaying your trip, but keep your eyes on Me and don't look back. I will show you the way. Don't worry about how you will get there. I will coordinate every step and show you your destination. The pace has already been set to your destined place of honor. I am truly pleased with you and have never doubted your return. My love for you is great. Stand firm and be of good courage. I am always present with you. Please hear Me my child. Hear Me and believe."

The music and the dancing suddenly stopped. His voice echoed and faded in the whistling wind, disturbed and awakened in the night by the blaring of nearby sirens. Startled, Jalena sat up in bed.

"Oh, God! Was I dreaming? No! It was so real. Oh, my God. I've never ever had a dream like this before. It had to be real...was it? Was it a personal message from you? Just for me? It was amazing and prophetic. I danced with you and the angels! I can still hear the music and You speaking to me...Your voice...the words are still playing over and over in my ears. Oh, Lord, my God. I need to get this down in my journal, but the tears are blinding my eyes. I have to write it...your message was just for me. I have to remember every word You said. Let me remember! Thank you...thank you, God! I hear You! I hear You, and I believe.

Chapter 17

The next morning as Jalena sat in a neighborhood coffee shop, she was still in awe and feeling the effects of her dream encounter. She sat there thinking of how realistic it was.

Wow! I actually danced with God, and He talked to me! My heart is so overwhelmed. I have to stop these tears. People will think something is wrong with me - it's just so hard to stop thinking about it. He loves me. How can He love someone like me...but He does; He said so. Life has been so good, and I can't help but think about what's coming next. That dream answered so many questions and opened the door to the realm of my future. I'm so excited and want to tell everyone about it. But, for right now...best to keep it to myself - at least for now. Thank you, Father God. Sighing, she took a sip of water.

I better make the most of this day since it's back to work for me tomorrow! Her thoughts were then interrupted by the waitress.

"Ma'am, may I take your order?"

"Yes, I'm so ready, but can I first ask you a quick question?

"Yes, ma'am.

"Is that a clinic across the way? I see a lot of people going in and out; it reminds me of a place that was a part of my past."

"Yes, ma'am. It's the new free clinic; many people who have no medical insurance end up there. They also have a blood donation program. Some people go to get their daily dose of methadone and sad to say, there are others who are being treated for HIV and AIDS. My cousin, Damien, was in and out of that place for methadone and HIV treatments. Last year, he died of AIDS."

"Oh...so sorry for your loss."

"Thank you. Can I take your order now?"

"Yes...thanks! I'll have two scrambled eggs, grits, rye toast and a cup of green tea with two sugars and lemon, please."

"Yes, ma'am. I'll be right back with your order."

"Thank you."

Wow! Thank you, God. Even though I used drugs, I'm free of addiction. I almost ended up in a place like that. It was a pathetic life. That could be me. I could have been one of them...in that building....suffering with a horrible addiction! Father, I'm so grateful to You. Thank you for grace and mercy.

Jalena continued watching as people walked in and out of the big, gray stone building. Something then caught her eye.

Wait! Is that Delia Morgan going in? I'm having trouble making out her face...I do have 20/20 vision...that is her. But, she looks so - so thin and so sickly.

Jalena jumped up from her seat and ran towards the door and said, "Miss, I'll be right back. You can just set my food on the table. I have to check on something real quick."

"Oh...okay, ma'am."

Stepping outside the doors she looked, straining her eyes and said, "That is Delia but not the Delia I remember. She's lost so much weight and looks so... She can barely make it up the street. I need to catch her before she goes into that building. Delia! Delia! Delia Morgan!"

Delia, never hearing Jalena's voice continued into the clinic. Failing to get her attention, Jalena walked back into the restaurant with thousands of thoughts racing back and forth in her now confused mind.

Dang, she didn't hear me. She got away before I could catch her. Wow! What's wrong with her? What happened to Delia? She's really changed since the last time I saw her with Jared.

She's lost so much weight. It's not a healthy look. No diet did that to her. I should go in and talk with her? Mmm...or maybe not. She won't want to talk to me anyway - seeing the way I treated her. I'm so sorry about that. I'm so ashamed and disgusted with myself. I have to apologize for the way I acted. I have to.

Chapter 18

"**N**umber 36. 36? Is Number 36 here?"

"I'm here! Please just give me a chance to get there."

Delia's number was called. It was her turn to see the physician on call. After months of not feeling well and not knowing what was wrong, she was referred to the clinic. Not having proper health insurance was a real barrier and caused a great delay in getting the aid she needed so very badly.

Thinking it was the Mononucleosis she'd contracted in high school rearing its ugly head again, she rested and dealt with it in her own way. Delia got through it before and felt as if she'd be able to handle it this time too. No longer was she able to take the pain. With things no better, a good friend suggested she go to the clinic and get help. Today she was a patient at the Community

Health Center clinic...number 36 in line. Weakness constrained her thinning body as she made her way to the physician's assistant.

"Have a seat while I get some additional information. You okay?"

Delia harshly answered saying, "Do I look okay?"

She sat down on the brown, wooden, rickety chair in the corner of the stark white room. Unfazed, the very stern looking woman got right down to the business at hand.

"Your name?"

"Delia Morgan."

"Is there a middle initial?"

"T...Theresa"

While the information was being taken, a nurse came over to Delia and said, "Let's get your vitals and take your temperature. You're feeling quite warm."

A thermometer was placed in Delia's mouth. An awkward silence took place as they waited for the result. After a moment, the nurse removed it and said, "Let me see. Yes, you do have a fever."

Completing the information with the assistant, Delia sat in a wheelchair and was taken into a private room where the nurse handed her a gown and sheet.

"Put this gown on. Place this sheet over your lap. The doctor will be in soon. Would you like a magazine to read while you wait?"

"No...no, thank you."

Weak and tired of being sick, Delia took her time getting undressed and changed into the blue-checkered gown. Finally changed, she used every ounce of strength she had to boost herself up onto the examination table. Placing the sheet upon her lap, she lay down and waited patiently for the doctor to enter the room.

I'm so sick of this. I wish I'd come in before everything got so bad, she thought as she looked up at the posters and framed pictures that were sequentially placed on each wall of the small, white room. After a while, there was a knock on the door, and the doctor entered.

"Hello, Miss Morgan. My name is Dr. Alexander. I've been looking over your symptoms here on your chart very carefully. I've some major concerns. You've stated that there's been a lack of energy and you've lost quite a bit of weight in just over a month. With a 102-degree fever, we're going to give you a fever reducer. You've also stated that you've had frequent nausea, abdominal cramps and vomiting. How often do you have these yeast infections?"

"More than I'd like to admit. It seems like it never ceases. I'm just so tired of it all, Doctor. I feel so dirty and

want whatever this thing is gone! Please give me something...anything."

"Miss Morgan, I have a sensitive question for you.
Have you ever been tested for HIV?"

Shocked by his question, Delia hesitantly said, "No - I
haven't. Why? Do you think that's what I have? No,
Doctor Alexander! No!"

Placing his hand on her shoulder, he said, "Now calm
down, Miss Morgan. I can't say anything for sure, but I'd
like to at least take some blood and check it out. In the
meantime, I'd like for you to get this prescription filled
downstairs. The nurse will give you a few extra samples
to take with you. We're going to rush the lab for results.
Let me check your vitals one more time and then you can
go home and rest. You'll get a call when the results come
in."

"Doctor, I've had Mononucleosis. Couldn't it just be a
severe case of that?"

"Yes, I see it listed here on your chart. It's a possibility. I'm having it checked. But just to make sure we're not
missing anything, I'd also like to have you tested for
HIV."

Delia was beyond worried and was trying to hold
back tears that were now burning and blinding her eyes.
How could this be? She thought as she tried to hide fear
and anxiety that was ready to explode within. Memories

of a past incident flashed in her mind. A lonely tear fell and hit her hand as the doctor continued talking and examining her. Delia's mind was blank to his words of consolation. She stopped listening and was wondering about what the future would hold for her if she were to have full blown AIDS.

"Listen, I don't want you to worry about this, Ms. Morgan," he calmly said.

"It's so easy for you to say," Delia sharply said as she wiped away tears.

"I'm only saying that right now—why worry? We don't have the test results. It may not even be HIV. In all likelihood, it is the Mononucleosis as you've said. Please, let's not put any more stress on yourself by worrying; stress will only make you sicker. Okay?"

"Okay...I guess."

"Miss Morgan, do you believe in the power of prayer?"

"I don't know. Never really do any of that."

"You might just want to try it out. It helps me. I do believe in the power that comes from the Man Upstairs. Get dressed now. Give this paper to our receptionist and go down to the pharmacy and get this prescription filled. As soon as we hear anything, I'll personally call you. We need to get you back to a normal, healthy state. Are you okay with that?"

"Yes, Dr. Alexander, I definitely am."

Chapter 19

It was long and stressful day for Jalena, especially after seeing Delia. The reality of what she saw weighed heavily on her mind. She tried putting it to rest, but it was hard to block the feeling and emotion.

What's wrong with her? I really need to talk with Jared to see what he knows. But first I need to call mom and see how she's doing.

Before she could pick up the phone, it rang.

"Hello."

"Hey, Girl! This is your long lost, forgotten about friend, Sharina!"

"Sharina! How are you?"

"Just calling to check on you, Sis. How are you? Sorry I didn't get to be with you at Trisha's service. I heard it was a nice tribute."

"Oh, I'm good. Just keep'n busy, is all. Moms out of town. She's away in Florida, visiting relatives."

"So you're alone. Do you need company?"

"No. I'm good. Sharina, let me run something by you."

"Sure. What is it?"

"Remember a while back I was telling you about that girl, Delia Morgan that Jared was hanging with?"

"Yeah. You told me about how rude you were to her and—"

"Let's not discuss that part again, Sharina. But anyway, today was the first time I've seen her since that day. I was sitting in the restaurant across from that new clinic on Taylor Street and saw her."

"Oh yeah. I hope you did your due diligence and apologized for your behavior, Jalena."

"No...didn't get a chance to."

"And why is that, my friend?"

"Sharina, will you let me finish! Geez!"

"Okay...okay, but the Bible says—"

"Sharina! I didn't get to talk to her!"

"Jalena, stop yelling. I'm listening."

"Well finally. I didn't get to talk to her. I called out to her, but she didn't hear me before she walked into that clinic. You should have seen her. I couldn't believe it. She looks like she's anorexic."

"Seriously?"

"Yes! Just thinking about her and what I saw makes my bones quiver. That poor girl looks like she's really suffering...and why was she going into that clinic?"

"Well, you just said she looked sickly."

"I know but, she must have some type of medical and health benefits. Most of the people who go there are either drug addicts or have... No! No! It can't be! No! I refuse to even think this way. There's no possibility!"

"What? What is it Jalena?"

"Sharina, I have to go. I'll talk to you later. Bye!"

Before Sharina could respond, Jalena quickly ended the call.

"Dear God, please don't let it be! Jared was dating her! Oh, God! No! I've got to call him right now. Where's my cell phone? Where's my phone? My purse. It's in my purse. Dang, I keep meaning to clean this thing out...can't find a thing in it. Here it is. Okay, let me think. What's his job number? Hmm...okay...5403225. Shoot! Why am I getting a freakin' recording? Come on! Jared, pick up...Pick up the phone! I don't want to speak to an answering machine...please pick up...somebody, please pick up the dang phone!"

Jalena sat down. "Okay...okay, he's not picking up. Why am I letting fear rise up in my spirit? I really need to calm down and quickly. My mind is racing all over the place - so many thoughts are playing tricks with my mind".

She sat back, closed her eyes and took a deep breath and began thinking calmly, *Okay, Jalena. Take a deep breath and calm it down. You don't even know if the girl has the AIDS virus, and here you are in panic mode. Let it go! Jared will be home soon. Besides what good is calling him while he's on the job going to do. Just wait till he gets home. Now go cook dinner.*

She calmed herself, but was like an out of control crazy woman, who was once more holding her own private conversation with herself.

"Okay, let me get into this kitchen...oven is pre-heated...seasoned pork chops are in the fridge. We'll have some mashed potatoes, green beans and biscuits. Where is he at? Dang! Now I'm talking to myself and having a big-time conversation with me, myself and I. My nerves must really be shot. This has really got to stop!"

Hearing the door slam, she yelled, "Jared? Jared, is that you?"

"And who else would you be expecting? Although I don't feel like myself."

"What did you say?"

"Oh...nothing."

"I was just getting ready to cook dinner, but first we need to talk."

"Hey, Sis, don't worry about fixing me anything to eat. I don't have much of an appetite."

"Why? What's wrong?"

"Oh...just feels like I've been trying to come down with the something."

Jalena stopped what she was doing and went right back into panic mode as she rushed into the living room.

Jared sat down and said, "Been feeling like this for the past few days. Tired, headache, can't eat, upset stomach, pain in my side. I don't know what's going on with me."

Trying not to explode and show her panic, Jalena said, "Past few days? Why haven't you gone to the doctor to get it checked out?"

"Just don't have the time...can't afford to take off work...just can't do it."

"Okay...okay." Jittering inside, she thought, *I have to keep a positive mind and not think what I'm thinking.*

Jalena looked at him and brusquely said, "Listen up, Jared Austin Mathesin, you are going to make time and right now. Put your jacket back on. I'm taking you to Urgent Care."

"Jalena, I really don't want to go right now. It's been a long day; I'm tired, and all I want to do is take a shower and get into bed."

Raising her tone a bit, she said, "Jared, I'm not taking no for an answer. We're going to Urgent Care now!"

"But Jalena!"

"Jared, don't make me call Mommy."

"Oh - so you're pulling the call Mommy card?"

Jalena was now looking at her brother with squinting, angry eyes and not letting up. This was his clue that she was serious and not having it. He would do what she said.

"Okay...okay...cool beans. I'll go. Just don't call Mom. I'm not going to ruin her vacation and have her worrying about me, trying to catch the first plane, train, bus or boat – whichever one will get her here the fastest."

"Okay then. Put on your jacket on and let's go."

Jalena breathed a sigh of relief. Although she wanted to tell him about Delia, she just couldn't do it - not at that time. Her first mission was to get him checked by a doctor and then reveal the news about Delia. If he thought he'd contracted the AIDS virus, it might make things worse for Jared. So she prayed silently as they drove to Urgent Care. *Dear God...*

Chapter 20

"It's mononucleosis with strep," the doctor said as he handed a prescription to Jared.

"The kissing disease? That's what's causing all this?" said Jalena, with a big grin on her face.

"Okay, Jalena, you're not going to let me live this one down – are you?"

"Jared, I'm just glad it's not more serious. I told you about those lips of yours."

"Here we go with the lip jokes. Please don't start with me, Sis."

"Dr. Wilson, what should Jared be doing to get rid of this?"

"There's really nothing that can be done about mono-nucleosis. What you can do is take a pain reliever for the headache. Fill that prescription for penicillin. It should get rid of the strep throat. Get plenty of rest, no heavy work, stay hydrated and eat healthy. I'll give you a note for your job; you should take the next few days off to rest."

"But, Doc...I—"

Doctor Wilson quickly interrupted his objection. "You are taking time off from work, young man. You're not going to feel better unless you do."

Jalena patted her brother on the back and said, "Thank you, Dr. Wilson. I was so worried about my baby brother."

"Come on, Jalena. I'm not a baby anymore."

"Well, sometimes you act like one, brother dear."

"Mr. Mathesin, I want you to see your regular doctor for follow up in a few days."

Jared shook the doctor's hand and said, "Thanks, Doc."

They left. Jared smiled at Jalena and said, "Are you okay now, Momma Jalena?"

"Yes, I am. At least we can leave with the peace of mind knowing that you are going to be okay. You really had me worried."

"Why were you so worried? I told you it was probably just the flu or something, nothing that serious."

"You are and you always will be my baby brother no matter how old you get. I have the right to worry if I want to. Besides, if Mom were here, she'd have done the same thing."

"Women! You're too much to handle. For crying out loud, can't a man be a man and take care of a little thing or two without you gettn' so emotional?"

"Jared, this wasn't just a little thing. I'm glad I forced you to go. Now we know the problem and how to treat it. First thing in the morning we have to get that prescription filled."

Driving down the brightly lit, tree lined strip, Jalena thought about Delia and got up enough courage to talk about it to her brother.

"I saw Delia Morgan today."

"Really? I haven't seen or heard from her in months. Where'd you see her?"

"I stopped to get breakfast at that little coffee shop over on Taylor Street. There's a new Community Health Center Clinic in the old Bradbury building?"

"Did you talk with her?"

"No, she was going into the clinic. Jared, she looked terrible. She looked sickly like maybe she had a disease or something."

"What are you talking about...disease. Are you sure it was her?"

"Yes, I'm positive. That clinic caters to HIV and AIDS patients."

Jared frowned and shook his head in disbelief. "Wow, J...hope you're wrong. If you'd only gotten a chance to know her, and given her a smidgen of a chance, you'd have found that she's a very nice person and not the slut that a lot of people have so wrongly shamed and accused her of. That rumor was started by an old boyfriend. She refused to give into him so he punished Delia. He and a few of his friends entrapped Delia at a party she went to. She was raped by him and two other guys who are now serving time in prison for what they did to her. She was so messed up after that...took years of therapy and the help of friends for her to break away from the guilt and pain she felt about getting caught up in that situation."

"Really? I never heard about that, Jared."

"Yeah. Remember the big trial involving the football players at Jeremiah Regional High? It was all over the news. The police got all up in that joint pulling students from classes, trying to get info. Parents were in an uproar about how their kids were treated."

Jared, slapped his hand on his thigh and said, "If she has AIDS, it's because of those boys who raped her."

When Jalena heard the truth about Delia, she felt even more guilt ridden and couldn't say a word as Jared pleaded Delia's case. Jared threw his head back and said, "Wow, Sis! Now I know why you were so frantic to get me to Urgent Care. You were thinking that if Delia had AIDS, I'd to be infected too. Am I right?"

Jalena kept her eyes on the road and winced. He was right. She had panicked at the thought that it had been a possibility.

"Sis, am I right? No need to play deaf."

"Yes...yes...you're right! It crossed my mind!"

"Jalena, it more than just crossed your mind. Listen to me and listen good: Delia and I never, ever slept together! Never even got to first base. I told you I was helping her with a project and that was the honest truth! We were messing with you...her holding onto my arm...me calling her my boo. You were set up and missed it! You messed things up when you started acting tough and talking down to her – you did that! It really hurt Delia's feelings! She cried when we got into the car and vowed never to come back into to our home as long as you were there. We ended up at the National Library when we left the house."

Jalena eyes began to water. "Jared, I'm so sorry for the way I acted. When I saw her today, I wished that I could erase and take back everything I said along with the way I acted. I'm just so protective of you that sometimes I forget and treat you like a child. I'm so sorry for not believing and trusting that you'd do the right thing. Please forgive me?"

"J, I did that a long time ago. I know you just want what's best for me. It wouldn't be right if you didn't; you're my sister. It's all good. It's all good."

Jalena remembered how Delia quoted that same phrase, "It's all good. It's all good," and the comment she made to Delia after that. When Jared said it, more salt was poured into her wounds and the burden of guilt that Jalena felt at that very moment. She was truly sorry for the way she acted and wanted to make amends with Delia. She wanted to find Delia if it was the last thing she ever did. She had to make things right.

Chapter 21

"Peters, Simon and Jacobs. This is Jalena. May I help you? He's not in today, Mrs. Bellchem. Is there anything I can help you with or would you like to be transferred to his voicemail? Yes, he will be in tomorrow. Yes, ma'am. I'll transfer your call to voicemail. Have a blessed day."

Jalena was back at work in a nice, quiet office; Laurie was out on a sick day. Mr. Peters was also out for the day, but left a task list to be completed by end of day. Jalena completed most of the work that could be done, so decided to take full advantage of the peace and quiet.

There was a lack of work and clients calling and coming in so she planned to see what could be done to make amends with Delia Morgan. Guilt hung heavily around her heart. She was unable to rest until she could do what was right. In years past, it had made no difference to

Jalena if she hurt someone's feelings. Whether it was physically or mentally, it made no difference to her. She was very abusive in tongue...did what she wanted and said whatever she felt. This was a major transformation for her - another step towards her own personal healing. She thanked God daily that she was no longer that hard-hearted person.

She had a new compassion for life and for others. Although there were still moments when the old ways seem to want to flare up, she knew how to control it and wouldn't allow it to control her before she'd get it in check, pray and ask God for His forgiveness. She would see Delia and make things right.

Before she left for work, it was a struggle, but she convinced Jared to give her Delia's address, which was only a few blocks away from her job. It was actually on the way home. Since it was a nice, cool spring day, she'd walk halfway and then catch the #2 bus the rest of the way.

While walking, she called Tahlia.

"Tahlia!"

"Jalena! How are you?"

"I'm great! We have to get together...shopping or maybe a movie?"

"For sure, why not, J. What've you been up to?"

"Well...right now I'm on my way to make amends."

"What? See that's what I'm talking about. That's what real god-like transformation is all about! Who are you making amends with?"

"I need to make things right with a friend of Jared's. I was very rude to her and I need to clean it up. I just hope it's not too late to straighten things out."

"Jalena, it's never too late for something like that! Where do you have to go?"

"It's in the 300-block of Clyburn. The first thing I'll have to do when I see her is apologize for my bad behavior and pray that she's forgiving. It bothers me to know that I caused her to cry because of the way I acted."

"Oh, J...really! You were that awful to her?"

"Yes, I was, Tahlia. I'm going to have to get a grip on things and really think before I speak. I have a new image to uphold. I can't emulate God and represent Him in a favorable manner that's unpleasing to Him. He's with me and in me, and I have to show up for Him; I have to glorify Him. Besides, He's my new dance partner".

"Preach, Sister Girl...preach! Listen to you! I am so proud of you!"

Inwardly, Jalena was smiling. She couldn't stop thinking about the dream and the way she was floating with smooth dance steps -- dancing with the King -- and how He whispered the plan for her life into her ears. It was something she'd never forget in a million years. That dream greatly changed her outlook on life. She'd continue to keep it quiet and not tell her friend. For now, it was only between her, God and the angels.

"Okay. I'm here, Tahlia, I have to go. Maybe we can get together this weekend. Call me!"

"No, J. You call me! Okay?"

"Alright. Talk to you later! Bye!"

Looking up, she remembered that Jared said it was number 357...the two-story brownstone apartment building, sitting on the corner. She loved the beige window trim and the brown awning over the main door.

Her mind wandered to the future as she thought, *Wow! I'd like to have a brownstone house one day with a big backyard like that one. It has plenty of room for children and —*

"Whatcha doin?"

A small child came out of nowhere and ran right into Jalena as she was looking up at the building. Startled out of her thoughts, she felt the push, followed by a tugging on her jacket. The child was about five or six years of age. At first when she looked down, Jalena was perturbed that the girl had such boldness to approach a complete stranger. Then Jalena realized she should be gentle with the child - just in case a parent or someone was sitting and watching their interaction.

Just then a voice bellowed from the brownstone apartment building, "Lindsey! What did I tell you about walking up to complete strangers and talking to them? Girl, get your butt in this house! Get in here right now!"

Just hearing the intensity of the voice, Jalena knew this child was in store for either a spanking or some kind of punishment. Apparently, the child knew it too. Big drops of tears flowed down her cheeks and she began screaming loudly before she even hit the stairs of the brownstone. Jalena felt sorry for her; a good spanking was more than likely awaiting that little one.

The woman with the big brash voice yelled out to Jalena, "Who are you? What do you want? And who are you looking for?"

Not wanting to seem suspicious, Jalena quickly answered, "My name is Jalena and I'm looking for Delia Morgan. Does she live here?"

"Second floor, apartment B4 at the end of the hall, but I don't think she's been here for a few days. They say she's in the hospital. Excuse me one second. Girl, get in your room right now. What'd I tell you about talking to strangers? You just wait! Ooh...just wait! Imma get that tail in just one minute!"The little girl's cries were even louder.

Returning to the conversation, the lady said, "Sorry 'bout that. Yeah, they say she's in Maryland General Hospital, really sick. May not make it from what I hear."

Getting this information shook Jalena to the core. "Thank you, ma'am! I really appreciate it."

"Oh, you're welcome. Are you kin?"

Jalena quickly respond, "No, just a friend." As she walked away, burning tears welled up in her eyes. She felt a great burden in her heart for Delia and what she was going through. Somehow she'd get to the hospital to see Delia.

Chapter 22

"Hi, Jared."

"Hey, Sis. What's up?"

"Just calling to see how you're doing. Are you feeling better?"

I'm feeling better. I guess the medicine has started kicking in. I lay in bed for a while this morning, but was just too restless. I got hungry and I was able to keep a bit of food down. It feels good to feel better. Thanks for making me go to Urgent Care."

"I'm glad you're better. You can't have me worrying about you like this anymore. It's not normal and not good for my health." They laughed.

"Okay, okay...gotcha."

"Good. Jared, you know Mom returns from Florida tonight."

"Yeah, I know. I'm glad she'll be home and even happier that she was able to take the time and visit Uncle Carl and Aunt Cece in Kissimmee."

"I know. It was long overdue. That senseless argument over grandma's Will caused so much turmoil and strain on their relationships. I'm glad everyone got their share of Whatever and everything's been resolved. We have to make sure things are ready when she gets home. The house needs to be spotless. Dinner should be on the table when she gets there. I'll be home as soon as possible so we can work it out."

"Sis, don't worry about it. I got it."

"Jared, you're supposed to be resting."

"J, I'm fine. My headache's gone. I'm taking the meds, and won't do any heavy lifting. I got this."

"Are you sure?"

"Yes, I'm sure."

"Well, I guess that'll be okay – just be careful. You clean...I'll cook. After dinner, I need to run an errand. I'll tell you about it when I get home."

"Okay, Sis. See ya."

"Okay. Love you!"

"Love you more, Sis!"

<><><>

As Jalena entered the house, she was met with the fresh scent of pine - clean and fresh smelling. She almost slipped on the wet, drying floor.

"Jared!" No answer.

Again she yelled. "Jared!"

Walking further into the house, she found him hard at work, still mopping the floor, with headphones apparently listening to music blasting within in his ears.

Once again, she yelled, "Jared!!! Jared!!"

She tapped him on the shoulder and finally had his attention.

"What the--! Jalena, you know better than to sneak up on me like that. Almost made me wet my pants!"

"Sorry. I tried, but you were so into the music and mopping. Hey, I can create a new dance...music 'n mopp'n...music 'n mopp'n. She laughed and began demonstrating. Jared wasn't laughing nor was he impressed. He turned his back and continued working. Jalena stopped the antic, cleared her throat, got serious and said, "This place looks and smells so good! Thanks, Jared."

Getting in front of him, she smiled and said, "Are you sure you're not overdoing it? Remember what the doctor said?"

There was only once in life when Jared stayed mad at his sister. Other than that, he could never stay mad - he valued their relationship. He returned the smile and said, "I'm not overdoing it. I just couldn't continue lying in bed doing nothing, knowing that the house needed cleaning."

"Well, I'm glad you're better, especially today. It means less work for me. Mom will be happy to know she has two responsible young adults living in this house."

Hanging her jacket in the closet, Jalena said, "I was able to work a half day today...had to run a few errands. I wanted to get here and get things in order, but you've taken care of the greater part. Thanks, Jared."

"No problem. It's my responsibility, too. Oh yeah, Mom called and said her plane gets in at 3:15 and don't bother cooking anything special for her. She ate like a pig this week and decided to do another one of those colon cleansing jobs. These are her words, Sis. 'need get all the crap out of my system.'"

"Oh, no! Not that!"

"Yes, that. You know how it goes and you know exactly what that means, J. She's been doing the same thing for a couple of years. Whenever she returns from a vacation, it's colon cleanse time."

"Why did I not remember that? Well, I guess we'd better enjoy this fresh, clean smell while it lasts because once she gets started with that cleansing, all bets are off. Certain rooms in this house will be off limits.

They laughed hard. Tears rolled down their cheeks.

"We might as well get our minds set and used to the fact that this is a yearly scheduled event...a part of life." Jared laughed even harder.

"Yeah, I guess so...oh well."

Jalena walked into the living room and sat down on the window seat while Jared finished cleaning. She reminisced about her day and thought about Delia. Plans were made to visit the hospital once Mom was settled in. In her mind, she wished the hands of time could be rewound. There were a lot of things she'd handle differently - things that disturbed her life. There were some good times and some really, tearful times. She was finally able to admit that there was no one to blame but herself.

Sitting quietly, she thought about the night when the devastation of her life came to a head. It was the darkest and most angriest time for Jalena. She'd isolated herself from the life she knew. Depression and the influence of a gang caused her to retreat and turn away from her loving family.

Prior to that, everything was good. She had a job as a front desk clerk at Roxy Cleaners. There was a little bit of money in her pocket every day. But then she met MD -- Moses Dorin. They called him MD not only because of his initials but also for what his initials stood for in other terms: medical doctor. But this unofficial MD always had whatever anyone needed for whatever pain he or she was in. It didn't matter what it was, MD had it.

On the streets, he was also known as the medicine man. Just like Moses in the Bible, Moses Dorin could lead someone to the Promised Land with a pocketful of miracle-working meds.

Jalena met him just after her dad died while working at the cleaners. She was suffering with tremendous emotional and mental pain. Since MD was a regular customer at the cleaners, they frequently talked. He made her laugh. She was comfortable with him and getting to know MD, she trusted him.

After they became friends, he offered Jalena his "medical" help. He'd be hanging out at a friend's house where they'd meet. It didn't take long. Before she knew it, Jalena was flying high. All of this was new to her and it felt good. She no longer had to think about losing her dad and how she wasn't present when he died. The pain of missing him was sometimes unbearable. He was her buddy, but was now gone. With MD's help, she found solace in the feeling she got when on a high; MD was her savior.

At night, when she got home, Jalena went straight up to her room and hid until the next day. Marinda and Jared had no idea that Jalena was deep into drugs. They knew there was a problem, but just thought she was tired from going to school and then going straight to work. Hiding the truth, she slept off the high and was right back at it the very next day.

She was faking her school attendance. Jalena was handing in homework assignments she'd got from her friends and then going to school when she felt like it. More often, she skipped school and headed over to the hotbox, which was what they called the hangout.

The night before this gang busted into their home, Jalena was with them and began giving out a little too much personal information about things in their house. She bragged about her dads watches that were left behind after he died and must have even mentioned where they were in the house. The next thing she knew, they were making plans to seize the jewelry. Jalena tried to stop their efforts, but it didn't work. They wouldn't listen to her.

She was never officially part of the gang, but hung around with them so much that they decided to give her the name, "Little Sis" and she loved it. It made her feel wanted. She belonged to this new family. When with them, she'd forget about her problems. MD with his feel good meds also helped to take away pain when she slipped back into phases of depression.

Jalena was truly in love with feeling high. It was like candy to her. So on this particular night, they gave Jalena some candy just to shut her up and stop any attempts at getting them to stay away from the house. She was desperate to stop the plans that were made, but was so high she slept till the next day and never made it back home until everything was over and done with.

Someone must have mentioned her name during the break-in. When she got home the next day, Jared's anger was not hidden. He was so angry with Jalena that he threw her up against the wall as he told her everything that happened. Pinning her up against the wall, he said, "If I hadn't come in when I did, Mom might have been killed."

Then he told Jalena to get her things and leave. He yelled at her and said, "Dammit, Jalena! You're going to learn the hard way! Since you love the streets so much, get your things and go! Get out of here!"

At first she thought he was just kidding. This was her brother...her little brother. He couldn't really mean what he was saying. So Jalena tried hard apologizing with tears streaming down her face. He wasn't fazed by her demeanor. He wouldn't hear her. It meant nothing to him.

So he screamed, "The safety of my family comes first. You're not going to put us in harm's way anymore. It's time for you to make up your mind. What are you going to do? You love the streets so go live on the streets. Get your stuff. Get whatever you need and get out of here now!"

Marinda came down the stairs and didn't say a word. She just looked at Jalena and turned around and went back up the stairs. You could see all of the bruises on her face and arms. Jalena knew that it was time for her to leave.

Jared then threatened her, "If you don't leave right now, I'm calling the police. You just better thank God that Mom didn't press any charges against you - I will!"

Jalena felt so bad. She was guilt-ridden. Her mind was filled with discombobulated thoughts. How could this be happening to me? What was I thinking?

Sadly, she walked away. After leaving, Jalena stopped by the police station and gave names, places and descriptions. All of the gang members were booked and charged that same night. Thank God for favor, for they never found out that it was Jalena who pointed the finger.

Now back, in the cozying love of home, she sat there with her daunting memories. Thinking back on those brutal days brought tears to her eyes. Jared and her mom had forgiven her. She was no longer the same person as she was back then. Jalena was clean and whole in my mind, soul, spirit and body.

Lost in those memories, Jared brought her back to reality, snapping his fingers in her face.

"What's up, Sis? Where were you just now? You seemed like you got caught up in something and left me for a while. What's going on?"

Wiping away tears, she said, "Oh...just thinking about life...past stuff."

"Hey, Sis...don't go back to that place. It's not worth the mental turmoil and anguish. That was then, this is now. Let's just be happy about life as it is today at this very moment in time. Okay?"

"Yeah, you're right; this part of life is what really counts. You know, though, I was really feeling bad about what you told me concerning Delia and how I made her cry. Jared, you just don't know how bad I feel about that. I went over to her apartment to apologize."

"I figured that was the plan when you asked for her address. How did she take it?"

"I didn't get to talk to her. A lady in the building says that she's in Maryland General Hospital and that it doesn't look too good for her."

"Really? Did you get to the hospital?"

"No, not yet. I knew Mom would be in today. I wanted to make sure everything was all set for her. I made arrangements with Sage to get Mom at the airport since he works over that way and then he's going with me to the hospital. I just hope it's not too late when we get there."

"You think I can hang with the two of you? I'd like to see her."

"Sure, if you don't mind being the third wheel. Once we leave the hospital, we're going over to the ITahlian Garden Buffet. I'm sure Sage won't mind."

"Now you know me. Food, especially at that buffet? Get me my plate so I can sit down and get my grub on!"

"Calm down, Jared. Are you sure you're going to be able to stomach all that food with being sick and all?"

"You may be right about that, but we'll see what happens."

"Okay." Jalena said with a sigh.

"After Mom gets home, we'll leave here around five. I'm really anxious to see Delia."

Chapter 23

"May I have your attention please? Flight 1006 has been delayed arriving from Orlando, Florida, due to severe weather. We'll give you an update as soon as any information is available. Thank you for your patience."

Sage sat waiting at the airport when the announcement was made. "Guess I'd better call Jalena and let her know what's going on. Can't have her worrying," he whispered to himself.

Dialing her number, he waited for her to pick up. "Come on, J, pick up the phone, baby. Pick up the phone."

"Hi, Sage, did you get Mom?"

"Hi, babe, I'm here at the airport. They're saying there's a flight delay because of severe weather in Orlando."

"Really? Let me see if I can get in touch with her and see what's going on. I heard that it was a little windy but not to this extent to cancel any flights. This worries me. As it is, she's not that fond of flying."

"That's right. I remember you mentioning that to me."

"I'll call her, Sage and get right back to you."

"Okay, I'll wait a little while to see if anything develops." Trying to stay positive and not worry about her mother's safe return, Jalena nervously dialed her number. Ever since Jalena's cousin Breanna was killed in a plane crash, they were all been a little nervous about flying. Breanna was only 22 years old and on her way to Bermuda for a vacation with friends. The night before her trip, Breanna called and asked Jalena if she could borrow a small traveling bag.

"Hey, Cuz. I'm ready for my trip to Bermuda! Yay! Finally getting away from all of the hassle at work."

"Breanna, I wish I were going too! Can I stowaway in your bag?"

"Jalena, I wish you were going with me. You know how crazy the two of us can be together."

Breanna picked up the bag from the house. They hugged and that was the last interaction Jalena had with her cousin. The plane never made it to Bermuda.

Jalena was now desperate to speak with her mother. She finally got through to her.

"Hello, Mom? Where are you? What are they saying?"

"Hi, Jalena. I thought I'd be home by now, but hurricane-force winds are blowing. They're saying it may not be safe for us to fly out tonight. We've been given hotel vouchers for rooms in the hotel right here at the airport and they've started booking flights for some time tomorrow."

"Okay, Mom, that sounds good. Are you all right with that?"

"Yes, but you know me and being in the air. My mind had me thinking all kinds of horrible things about flying out tonight. I was really getting nervous about it. This delay works well for me. I need to get a handle on this fear demon and ask God to take it away."

"Mom, please don't worry about it. Just enjoy the hotel along with every amenity it has to offer and get a good night's rest. What's that Scripture you always remind me of when I'm feeling fearful? God has not given you a spirit of fear—"

"Now listen to you, my little preacher girl."

"Stop it, Mom. I'm just reminding you of what you're always saying to me."

"I know, but it feels good to hear you remind me of the word of God. He has not given me a spirit of fear but has given me power, love and a sound mind."

"Yes, that's the verse. Now please don't worry. You'll have me worried if I know you're down there stressed, so promise me you won't."

"I won't. We'll just keep praying."

"Okay. Sage is waiting for you at the airport here. I need to call him back and let him know what's happening. As soon as they let you know your flight number and exact time the plane will be flying out, please let me know. Love you, Mom."

"Love you more."

Jalena immediately let Sage know the status. He left the airport, came straight to the house. They immediately left there to visit Delia.

Chapter 24

"**E**xcuse me please. Can you tell me which room Delia Morgan is in?"

"Let me see. Oh, here she is. Room D260 down the hall on the left. Make sure you put on a mask. You'll find it to the right side of the door; it's for the patient's protection."

"Nurse, what's her condition?"

"Are you a family member?"

"No, a friend."

"She's in stable condition. That's all I'm able to tell you."

Maryland General Hospital was a busy community hospital on Linden Avenue. This was not Jalena's first visit here. It was the same place where her dad made his transition. He was a smoker most of his life and he passed away from lung cancer. It was the one habit that he tried so hard to kick and succeeded in breaking only after he was diagnosed with the incurable disease. She remembered walking down these same bleak, white halls, hearing the same sounds and smelling the same smells.

It was a courageous walk for Jalena because she vowed to never visit this hospital again; the memories depressed her. This place had inscribed in her mind nothing but death. With each step, she relived the day so clearly, a day that would always be etched in her mind: April 1st. Yes, it is ironic that it happened on a day when people pull out their A-games to trick each other. On that day, she had a hard time believing that her daddy was gone. She remembered getting the phone call from Jared.

"J, you need to get to the hospital right away."

"Why, what's happening? Jared, what is it?"

"Dad's not going to make it. Get here as soon as you can."

"But—"

"J, just get here!"

When she received that call, Jalena was devastated. She cried all the way to the hospital. Her dad had been in the hospital for over three weeks and got worse instead of better. Breathing became difficult for him, so a machine was attached to help him breathe. Jalena had made it her true commitment to sit at his bedside every day and she did. But on that particular day, she was not able to be at his side; time was not her friend.

She tried hard to get there, but distance, transportation and traffic to the hospital were her opposition on that rainy April Fool's day. Since she had no car, it took her a great amount of time on the local bus. Traffic was horrendous in the late-day hustle of people making their way home with the five o'clock traffic. Since that time, she's felt an overwhelming guilt that on the day he passed away, she wasn't there. Conversations were cemented in her mind. With red, tear-filled eyes, Jared met her at the front entrance.

"Jared, where is he? Why aren't you in the room with Daddy?"

"Jalena, he's gone...Daddy's gone," he said letting his tears flow freely.

"No-oo, Daddy!" She cried. "Where is he? I want to see my daddy!" Jalena ran through the hallway and never stop until she reached his room. The lights were turned down, and the curtains were closed. As she approached his bed, Jalena said, "God! Why??" She cried so hard and feeling dizzy, she almost passed out. Jared grabbed Jalena and sat her down in the chair next to his bed. She touched his hand and then laid her head upon his stilled chest while the tears flowed. She took a last real look, up close and personal at every part of his face.

Jalena didn't want to forget. She wanted every feature and every line of his beautiful face ingrained in her mind. For some time, she sat there weeping silently in the dark. Satisfied, she kissed the cheek of his cold body.

She learned to cope with her father's death, but the pain of that day remains a constant reminder that she was not there in time. Now, here she was in the same hospital, breaking a vow to herself and not knowing what she would find when getting to Delia's room. She didn't want to face this same scenario.

Jared didn't make the trip to the hospital. He changed his mind. He was fearful of seeing Delia in her present condition and didn't want to stir up any old memories of his Dad. He was in a good place and he didn't want to dredge up the old stuff and bad emotions, so he made the choice to renege.

Jalena tried not being angry with him, but said to Jared, "What about me? What about my feelings? How do you think I'm going to feel when I have to walk back into that place?"

He just shrugged it off, walked away and said, "Sage will be with you."

Although Sage was in the building, he wasn't with her. He ran into one of his old professors on the main floor and was asked about serving an internship once he completed his residency. Jalena convinced him that she would be okay and encouraged him to stay and talk to Professor Beavers, who was also head of pediatrics. This would be a great opportunity for Sage.

It all came down to one important fact: she needed to face Delia alone and make peace with her. It was a good thing that original plans didn't work out with either Jared or Sage. She felt it was in God's plan for her to go this one alone. She'd have to shake off any past hospital memories. Jalena was forced to come to a new realization. Her life had changed - she was no longer the same. There were things in her past that at some point in her life would come back to haunt her. This was one of them. Here was a moment in time where she would have to face reality and learn to deal with this situation and others that she alone had caused.

Holding a crystal vase filled with red Roses, she arrived at D260 and grabbed a blue mask out of the metal box that was attached to the side of the door. She placed it over her mouth and took one scary, giant step into reconciliation as she crossed over the threshold into Delia's room.

"Delia?" She whispered.

Delia slowly turned her head to see Jalena as she approached her bed. It seemed, at first as if Delia didn't recognize who she was. Straining her eyes to see, she then said, "Jalena? What are you doing here?"

She was afraid to respond. Delia appeared to look even worse than when Jalena first saw her going into the clinic. Walking up to Delia's bed, Jalena shyly said,

"I heard that you were here in the hospital and wanted to stop by and visit."

Delia spoke softly. Her voice was weak, but strong at the same time. "Really. But why? Why would you want to visit me as rude as you were the last time you saw me? Jalena, you were not nice at all, so why in hell would you even want to show your face here today? Did you come to gloat? We're not friends or family. Why don't you just leave before I have you thrown out of here, and take your flowers with you. I'm allergic to both of you."

"Delia, please. Just give me a chance. Please?"

She looked at Jalena for a moment, breathed in deeply as if trying to catch her waning breath and said, "Okay, but say what you need to say and then please leave. I'm tired."

Jalena didn't want to waste time on any long explanations and said, "I've come to apologize for acting the way I did. I was out of line and it was uncalled for. You deserve to be angry at me. I acted like a pure fool. I'm so used to being overly protective of Jared, thinking of him as my baby brother. He's a grown man that I need to let go of and allow him to live his own life."

Moving closer to Delia's side, she sighed and said, "I heard some negative talk about you from a few people and instead of learning the truth, I let hearsay contaminate my mind and for that, I sincerely apologize to you. Delia, if you can find any space in your heart, will you please forgive me? I regret every nasty word and really need your forgiveness."

From the time the first word came from Jalena's mouth, Delia's eyes pierced through her and never moved or blinked. Something changed because as Jalena continued her plea, the angry lines in her face softened. Jalena knew that Delia was affected by the words that were said. She was glad that her words were heard and Delia didn't throw her out of the room. She had every right to, but she didn't.

With a cautious smile and a little more strength in her voice, Delia said, "You sound sincere enough and I believe you. I forgive you, Jalena Mathesin."

Jalena reached Delia's heart. She understood and forgave Jalena. Here it was again and still very simple. Three little words were said... "I forgive you." Without hesitation, Jalena was once again forgiven. She was once again free from the stress and guilt that she had placed upon herself by being unnecessarily mean to someone that didn't deserve it. Making the choice to forgive is freeing for both parties involved, and both Delia and Jalena felt a new found freedom on that glorious day.

Delia stretched out her weak hand to Jalena and asked, "Now, can you pour me a cup of water? My throat is parched and can you stay for a bit?"

Jalena's face brightened. She was happy to spend time with Delia. They talked as if they were bff's and Delia was the first person Jalena ever told about her dream. Delia was delighted to hear about it and asked her, "Do you think I'll be able to dance with God, too? Will He talk to me like He talked to you?"

Jalena became emotional when asked this question, but held on and answered Delia's question, "Most definitely, Delia, you will."

Delia smiled and suddenly turned her head away from Jalena. Both of them wiped away the tears that began to flow.

Delia then quickly turned back to Jalena and asked, "Will you pray with me and ask God to dance with me when I get there?"

Jalena tried holding back tears, but could not help herself as she took both of Delia's hands and prayed for her new friend. Jalena felt as if she would explode and tears were going to flood the room as they flowed. Both cried and believed that there would most certainly be a special dance moment arranged with God. A quiet peace filled the room that night. Jalena quietly left and Delia peacefully slept.

Chapter 25

The next day, Jalena was in prayer mode for her mother who was on her way home from Orlando and for Delia.

"Hi, Sage, did mom's flight come in yet?"

"No, not yet. I'm here at the airport now. I had some paperwork I needed to look over, so I figured I'd get here early and get my work done while waiting. The flight should be in soon. It's running on time."

"Okay, that's good. I'll be so happy to have her home. Remember now, her flight is coming in from Atlanta. That's where she transferred."

"Yeah, I didn't forget, babe. I'm sure she'll probably be glad to get here, too. Okay, I'm going to sit down and try to get some paperwork done. We should be there soon."

"Sage, I'm sorry I couldn't be there with you to pick her up. I should be done momentarily. Mr. Peters will be happy once I hand him these papers. I should be home when you and Mom get there. Once she's settled in, will you take me to the hospital again today? I want to go back and see Delia?"

"Yes, ma'am. I didn't get to see the pediatric ward last night. Professor said I could come back anytime and he'd give me a tour of the entire facility. Love ya."

"Love ya more, Sage. See you soon."

Sage found a seat in the noise filled airport. Looking around at all the commotion he thought, Man, I've got so much on my mind, it's hard to concentrate. Finals are coming up and although I want to practice as a pediatrician, I'm kinda having some second thoughts. I'm really struggling in my mind about which specialty of medicine I really want to practice. I need to know before I can apply for my residency. To top it off, I'm nervous about being alone in the car with Jalena's mom. This is the first time we've been alone together. Just why am I so nervous about this? Hmm...what time is it, anyway? Okay, I've got about ten minutes before her flight arrives. I need to relax and calm these fears. It'll be all right, Sage. It will be all right.

Just then, an announcement came over the loudspeaker, "Flight 1425 from Atlanta, Georgia is now arriving at Gate C10. Please make your way to meet your party at baggage claim C4."

Chapter 26

There she is. Okay, God, please let things go well with this drive home. Take away any fears I have. I'm a big boy. I can handle this. "Welcome home, Momma Marinda."

"Hi, Sage. Give me a hug. I need one after that flight."

Sage gave her the biggest hug he could muster up.

"Mmm, thank you, Son."

Sage tried make small conversation as they walked side by side.

"How was the flight?"

"Sage, it was nerve wracking. We had some turbulence for a little while off and on, but it finally settled down. I'm just glad to have my feet back on solid ground; I could kiss it."

Pointing at the baggage carousel, Marinda said, "Sage, there's my bag. It's the black one with red trim. Please catch it before it goes back around."

"Yes, ma'am."

Sage rushed over and grabbed her bag.

"Here it is. Only one?"

"Yes, I never carry a lot of baggage, as long as there's a washing machine and dryer wherever I'm going, it's not necessary to carry a lot of clothing and unnecessary bags. That's something you young people will learn sooner or later. It's not about what you wear, it's about how you wear it."

Beads of sweat formed on his forehead as Sage chuckled and said, "That's a good thing to remember. I'm going to have to put that one in my wallet and keep it. If you'd like to have a seat, you can wait here for me in the lobby while I go get the car."

"No, Son. Where is it? I'll walk with you."

Sage was hoping to have a little time to get himself together before the car ride. Still nervous, he answered, "It's on the lower level of the 'A' parking garage."

Marinda insisted, "That's not too far. I'll walk. I've been sitting a little too long. No good for these old knees," she said with a gleam in her eyes. Noticing the sweat on his forehead, she took tissues from her purse, patted his forehead dry and asked, "Son, why are you so nervous?"

This caught Sage off guard.

"There's no need for that. Calm down, Sage - calm down."

Sage took a deep breath and said, "Yes, ma'am. Are you sure about walking to the car? I can get it while you wait right here....won't take long."

"There's no need for that. I'm fine. Just let me grab hold to your arm as we walk. I'm still a little wobbly from that flight."

Sage began to feel somewhat relieved and comfortable with her holding to his arm. He began a conversation.

"So, how was your visit with the family?"

"You know, it was such a joy to see my brother and sister, even got to see some of my cousins and their children. I hadn't seen any of them in so long. They stopped talking to me over some silly tailed mess. You know how grown folk get when someone dies and leaves a Will? I got the house and they had a fit behind that. The thing is none of them ever came to visit or had any interest until Momma died. Now that's really silly. Isn't it?"

Thinking before he answered, Sage said, "I think I'm going to be careful in answering any questions before it gets me in trouble."

"No trouble here." They both laugh at him for trying to be so cautious.

"Where's Jalena? I thought she'd be here with you to meet me."

"She had to work some mandatory overtime. Her boss needed some contracts typed up at the last minute."

"Oh? Okay. My Jalena is such a hard worker. I'm so proud of her."

Finally making it to the car, Sage made sure she was seated in the car before he put her bag into the trunk. Getting into the car, he checked his rear view mirror and said, "Okay, let's get you home."

For a moment, there was an awkward silence as he drove out of the airport parking lot. After paying the attendant, Marinda got right down to business with a major personal question. "Sage, do you love my daughter?"

Before he could get his answer out, she continued with her query. "I need to know how you really feel about her and what your intentions are. Jalena has been through a lot, and I don't want to see my baby girl hurt by anyone, including you. If you don't have real intentions in making her a part of your future, I think she ought to know that before things get too deep between the two of you...if they haven't already."

Sage tried to recover quickly from what was said. He felt like he'd been hit with a one-two punch and said, "Momma Marinda, I love Jalena so much and have loved her deeply for a long time. I would never do anything to hurt her. I love her too much. In the past I admit that I have had a hard time with being committed only because of my fear of loss. I've been afraid to love because I'm afraid that if I love something too hard, too much and too fast that the love won't last long and will be taken away from me in some way. I have that awful fear. It all started with the loss of my parents. It's something that I've had to deal with for a long time and on my own. I've gradually been dealing with the fear and been a little nervous about talking to anyone about Jalena." She sat quietly and let him talk.

"Since you and I are here alone now, I'm glad you asked. I'm not afraid to let you know how I feel about her. I love her like I've never ever loved another woman; she is my first. Jalena is truly bone of my bone and flesh of my flesh, even before the vows have officially been taken. I love that girl, and I am asking you here and now for permission to marry her. I don't want to lose her; she means too much to me. I want her to be my wife."

As he spoke, tears rolled down his face. This was a serious conversation - one he never thought he'd be ready for. Feeling embarrassed for the tears, Sage was afraid to look in Marinda's direction, so he kept his eyes on the road.

She touched his hand and then spoke. You could clearly hear the tone of tears in her voice as she said, "Sage, I would have it no other way. You are already a son to me, and I'm excited to have you marry my daughter. This makes me happy, and I know that you'll make her happy as her future husband."

Marinda pulled more tissue from her purse and wiping away tears said, "Listen, I won't say anything about this conversation to her. When you get ready to propose, just let me know when the big day is going to happen. I'd like to prepare a celebration dinner on that same night."

"Thanks, Momma Marinda," he said with a smile.

Sage sighed with great relief. It pleased him that he was finally able to talk about his true feelings. It wasn't hard after all. Sage had Marinda's blessings, and it was now time to for him to take the next big step in making Jalena his wife for life. The conversation would now be easier as they traveled the rest of the way home.

Chapter 27

Early on Thursday morning, Delia passed away from complications due to pneumonia. Jalena felt sad, but believed in her heart that the daily visits helped Delia with her last days. Jalena smiled when she pictured Delia in the arms of God now dancing just as she did.

The Sunday before she transitioned, Delia said, "I want the eternal life that I read about in the Bible."

So Jalena called Elder Thomas, one of the hospital clergy, and they prayed with Delia as she gave her heart to God and received communion. Delia and Jalena hugged and cried when the ceremony was over and Elder Thomas assured her that she now had total salvation. He even gave her a certificate. Delia looked at it with pride written on her face. After he left, Delia handed that certificate to Jalena and proudly said, "Jalena, I want this to be buried with me in my casket."

Jalena did everything she could to contain herself and asked Delia why.

Delia smiled and said, "Just in case someone forgets to write my name down in the Lambs Book of Life, I'll have the proper certification to show them."

They laughed and then cried. Jalena knew Delia was serious about it so she made sure it happened. Helping Delia helped Jalena overcome some things that she'd been holding on to. The fear of the hospital was gone, and she became more lenient and patient with others. She learned to look within herself first and see her own faults. In the past, it was always someone else's fault when things were not going right. Now, she could acknowledge the right from the wrong and felt pretty good about being able to comprehend this when certain situations arose.

Wanting some relaxation of mind, Jalena stopped at the church on her way home from work, to see what her mom was so excited about in the thrift shop.

I'll give it a try, she thought. Who knows, I might really find something half way decent in the shop. As she exited the bus, Jalena was surprised to see Sage's car parked outside the church.

"Hmm, what's Sage doing here?" Not paying attention, she stepped up on the curb and almost tripped and fell but caught herself just at the right moment without injury and an embarrassment.

From outside, you could hear music from the church organ reverberating in the street and the choir singing high praises as they rehearsed selections for the next Sunday morning church celebration. Hands clapped and tambourines clanged. It sounded as if they were already in worship service.

Jalena decided to go in and listen for a bit before going into the thrift store. As she walked up the stairs into the sanctuary, she peeked in to see if she would be able to slide in without being noticed. There was no way that would happen. She was greeted by them as she walked inside, and then sat down in the very last pew.

The choir sang a joyous medley of songs, as the director stood near the back wall to check the sound that was resonating throughout the sanctuary.

They sang lyrics that rang throughout, singing, "Hallelujah! Sing praises to His name. He is the King of Kings and the Lord of Lords who reigns in heaven and rules the earth. I'll praise His name all the daylong and proclaim His greatness to show His worth. He is the great God."

Jalena clapped her hands and sang along with the choir and patted her feet to the beat of the music. This was just what she needed to end this day. It made her feel jubilant deep within. Maybe I'll get up enough courage to join the choir at the next rehearsal, she thought. Jalena left before they ended.

Her next plan was to see if she could find Sage. As Jalena walked through the vestibule, she met Mr. Hollins, the administrator and said, "Hello. Have you seen Sage?"

"Oh, I'm sure he left. He dropped off some great books. Can't wait to have them set up in our bookstore."

Jalena was disappointed to have missed him, but smiled knowing that he was just a phone call away.

She made it to the thrift store right before closing time. Jalena was in awe at what she saw. This wasn't your typical thrift store. If you didn't know any better, you'd think you were walking into a regular retail store, right off of Main Street. The decorations were classy with crystal chandeliers evenly lining the length of the brightly lit room. On one side, colored mosaic mirrors were beautifully designed on the cream-colored walls.

Clothing in every size and color were organized and neatly hung on store racks. In each aisle, accessories galore in every color were arranged on little glass, octagon-shaped tables in every section of the room. Jalena walked the aisles and noticed an array of church hats displayed by color and style in a section of its own.

"Wow! Mom was right. This really is a nice place," she whispered.

"We're just about ready to close, but can I help you?" The lady at the cash register politely addressed Jalena as she neatly folded a stack of pastel colored scarves laying before her.

"I guess I'm a little too late to really look around," said Jalena. "I'll return another day."

As she turned to leave, the lady said, "Wait a minute, aren't you Ms. Marinda's daughter, Jalena ?"

"Yes, ma'am."

"Girl, get over here! Don't you know who I am? You don't remember me? I'm Ms. Wallace. I used to be your Sunday school teacher."

"Ms. Wallace? Yes, it is you! Oh my goodness! I haven't seen you in so long. Please forgive me for not recognizing you."

"Come over here and give me a hug."

Jalena rushed over, excited to see the lady who had made such a difference in her life when she was a child in Sunday school. Ms. Wallace was the teacher who stuck up for Jalena and kept the boys from teasing her.

As a child, there was boldness to do certain things, but yet, Jalena suffered with shyness that at times over-ruled the boldness that was in her. It was her cross to bear. Most of the time she walked around with her head bowed low, afraid to look into the faces of persons as they talked with her. Gently, Ms. Wallace would take the tip of her finger and lovingly lift Jalena's chin, forcing her to look up and into her face when she spoke to Jalena. She was instrumental in helping to break that childhood propensity to look down.

"Oh, Ms. Wallace, I'm so glad to see you! When did you get back in town? I thought you'd moved to Texas?"

"I did. I moved to Dallas and still live there. I'm just here for a short visit with my sister, Evelyn. I'll be here for a couple of months or so. Evelyn is scheduled to have surgery next week, so I'll be here to help her out some. I'm so glad to see you, too! I'd heard you went through some rough times. I've been praying for you, dear. I knew you'd be back. I believe God's word when it says, 'Train up a child in the way he should go and when he is old, he will not depart from it', so I wasn't worried about you eventually finding your way back home to God and your family."

"Thanks for the prayers, Ms. Wallace. I truly needed them."

"Please girl, you are no longer my student. Please call me Rosalind and there's no need to thank me. Just doing my job as one of God's prayer warriors and ambassador for Christ," she said as she continued folding.

"Ms. Wallace—"

"Jalena, what did I tell you?"

"Oh...Rosalind," Jalena said with some hesitancy.

"I also want to thank you for how you taught me and protected me in Sunday school. I don't think I'd have made it had it not been for your care and concern for me. Even though I strayed when I got older, I often thought about you and how you protected me from some hurtful words. When I was living in the streets, I remembered that lesson you taught on the voice of God. There were times I had to open my ears and listen hard as I asked God to show me the way and tell me what to do. It was hard and I did some things that I ended up regretting, but I knew that someway and somehow, I would get out of it by God's grace and eventually be forgiven. Just knowing that really helped me to get through a lot of dark and lonely nights out there on my own. I thank you, so very much!"

"Jalena, it really blesses me to hear that and just knowing that through God, I touched your life. You've made my day, young lady, you really have. Sometimes it's good to hear testimonies like that. It helps to increase my faith in what I'm doing. I'm still teaching at church in Texas at The Greater Mount Olive Baptist Church of Dallas and loving every minute of it."

"Well, Rosalind, I really have to go now. Mom's probably wondering where I am. I know she'll be happy to hear that I finally visited the church thrift store, although I wouldn't call this a thrift store. They really need to change the name to something more classy."

"Yes, that would make sense. But for now, I need to finish up and close this beautiful place. I hope to see you again soon. Be praying for my Sis, okay? And you take care. I want you to always keep your head held high and let people see your beautiful face and smile. You're beautiful on the inside as well as outside."

With those words, she took the tip of her finger and lifted Jalena's chin higher and hugged her.

"Now leave here before you have me dropping tears. Love you, girl."

"Love you, too, Ms. Wallace."

"Rosalind?"

"Yes...Rosalind."

Chapter 28

J alena soon made it home after she stopped at the
market and picked up a quart of her favorite butter-
pecan ice cream.

"Mom, I'm home!"

"We're in the kitchen!"

Entering the house, she detected the sweet smell of
homemade, oven-baked biscuits. The only person in the
family who could ever make the taste buds dance the
happy dance with such savory delights was Aunt Jessie.
During family holiday gatherings, there was a big rush to
get those baking powder biscuits and her tasty sweet
potato pies. Some family members, including Jalena, hid
pies in a secret place to carry home at the end of the day.

"Biscuits!" Jalena shouted as she rushed into the
kitchen. There she was - Aunt Jessie, the younger sister of
Jalena's dad.

"Yes, the queen is present in this palace," said Jessie as she stood and greeted Jalena with opened arms and the warm hug that she alone could only give. It always made Jalena feel loved.

"How's my beautiful niece?"

"I'm good, Aunt Jessie," said Jalena as she put her ice cream into the freezer.

"Auntie, I'm feeling even better smelling those award winning, baking powder biscuits!"

Smiling, Jessie said, "I don't know about award winning. I just do the best I can, using my mom's old recipe. Although I've put my own spin on them, they're still just as tasty as I remember growing up."

"Well, they surely are the best...better than those things they call biscuits at the downtown chicken spot, Aunt Jessie."

Jalena took a seat at the table and asked, "Mom, is Jared here?"

"No. He's working overnight. He'll be home sometime mid-morning and I think I know why you're asking." she said with a smile.

"He won't be home tonight! Well, thank you, Jesus!" Jalena was in her glory and shouted, "That means more biscuits and molasses for me all mine!"

Jessie chuckled and said, "Girl, you are too silly. We need to make sure we save a few for my nephew. As a matter of fact, I may even drop some off to him at the job on my way home tonight."

"Aunt Jessie - there's no need for you to go out of your way...no need for that. What he doesn't know won't hurt him."

"Believe me, girl, it's not out of the way. Besides maybe I'll get a free oil change out of the deal."

"Aunt Jessie, what's the occasion? Why are you baking biscuits tonight? It's not Christmas, Easter or Thanksgiving. What's up with baking biscuits?"

Marinda quickly answered. "Let me take that question. Your Aunt has just informed me that she's moving away from here and taking up residence in Powder Springs, Georgia."

Jalena said, 'Powder Springs, Georgia' in unison with her mother.

"Jalena, how did you know?" asked Jessie.

"Sasha was here and told me. She's quite upset about the move, Aunt Jessie. She doesn't like the situation, but has resigned herself to the fact that it's happening."

Sighing, Jessie said, "I know she's upset, but it's something I have to do. I've wanted to make this move for a good while. It's a great opportunity for both of us. I'll be making thousands more and managing my own education office along with a college satellite program. I've been praying and asking God's favor and He did it. I believe in my heart that He's the one who opened up this big window and is pouring out this blessing for us. I can't let it opportunity pass by. Something like this may never come along again. Do you know that because of this job in the education system, Sasha gains a full ride scholarship at Georgia Tech, just thirty minutes away?"

Marinda gasped and said, "Oh my goodness, that's pure blessing. It's the opportunity of a lifetime. I guess Sasha, or better yet, all of us better get over your leaving here, Jessie."

"Aunt Jessie, does Sasha know about this? It's awesome? She didn't even mention it to me."

"No. She doesn't know. I just found out today when I got my clearance forms. I signed and submitted them this afternoon. Everything's set for us to leave the day after Christmas."

"The day after Christmas? That's only three months away! Sasha will be bummed."

"I know, but I have to do what's best for both of us. She'll get over it and make a lot of new friends. So we'll be flying out the day after Christmas. Matt is going to drive the car down sometime after the New Year. So honey, that's why I'm baking biscuits for you today. Don't know when I'll be baking them again. Things will be too busy for me to make any for the upcoming holidays. Just don't tell the rest of the family. They'll have to get some biscuits from somewhere else on their own. Maybe from the Colonel, Chicken Spot or the guy who loves spinach."

"Now that's not funny, Jessie," Marinda said. "I'll miss your biscuits, but miss you much more."

"Rinda, I'm going to miss you, too. We can visit each other from time to time, and we're only a phone call or a plane flight away."

"Airplane? Well...I guess," Marinda sadly said.

"Mom...Aunt Jessie, don't go getting all sad and mushy. We've got a good three months to have some fun and enjoy each other's company. I'll talk with Sasha and make her see what a blessing this is. But right now, let's just sit down and enjoy some of these biscuits with some butter and hot molasses."

"That sounds delicious to me! Now Marinda, you get the butter and heat up some molasses. Jalena, get the good china plates, saucers and tea cups. I'll check the biscuits in the oven and put water on for some Cinnamon tea.

"Yes, ma'am," Jalena said with a big grin.

Chapter 29

"**G**ood afternoon, Sir. Welcome to Zales®. My name is Thomas Ramsey and you are?"

"Sage...Sage Linendoll."

"So nice to meet you, Mr. Linendoll. How may I help you this evening?"

"I'm looking for a birthday gift for my girl. I want the perfect ring."

"An engagement ring? For her birthday?"

"Yes, Sir...an engagement ring."

"She's one lucky lady. When's her birthday?"

"Thursday. I'm taking her out for a nice dinner at the Citronelle in DC and then I'll take her back to her mom's home where her family will gather for cake and ice-cream."

"Sounds nice. So what's your budget, Mr. Linendoll?"

"I want something nice and classy looking for the most beautiful girl in the world. I need something in the $5,000 range or a bit over. I don't want anything too fancy or cheap looking, though."

"Come right this way and have a seat. Would you like a cup of coffee, tea or champagne before we get started?"

"No, thanks. I'm good."

"Okay, then. Let's get started." Opening up the glass case in front of him, Thomas pulled out a single ring. "Now this one is a 14K white gold. It has 100 stones and is 1.45 carat weight."

"How much, Mr. Ramsey?"

"You're in luck. The list price is $5,135.83, but today it's on sale for $2,187.48."

"Hmm, I don't know. It looks chintzy, and there's too much going on with it. I just don't know. I want to make the right decision. My Jalena loves simple things. That one looks like it'll take too much to keep clean. How about that one over there in the far left corner?"

"This one?"

"Yes. That's the one."

"It's a beauty...1-carat, certified diamond solitaire engagement ring in 14K white gold. Now it's a little bit out of your price range."

"Exactly how much out of range is it?"

"The original price was $7,499.00, and it's now on sale for $6,699.00."

As Mr. Ramsey talked, he placed the ring on a small, red-velvet pedestal for Sage to examine. He looked at the ring carefully and said. "It's nice - simple but elegant. It's a bit higher than what I'd planned on spending."

"I'll tell you what, Mr. Linendoll, since it's the last one we have in stock and I can see that this girl is pretty special to you, I'll let you have it for $5,999.00 so you can at least see the number five in the pricing." He laughed.

"Does that number include taxes, Mr. Ramsey?"

"For you, Sir, yes, it does."

"That's favor from God. Can you fit it to a size 6 by Thursday morning?"

"I believe this is a 6."

"That's even greater favor." Sage smiled and said, "I'll take it. This is going to be the best gift my love has ever had."

"Let me shine it up for you and put it in a beautiful box. It'll only take a moment."

"I'll have that coffee now," said Sage with a grin.

"Sure, I'll have my assistant bring you a cup."

Chapter 30

"Sasha, what's wrong? You seem a little off today. Are you not feeling well? What's up with you?"

Holding back tears, Sasha, said, "Krystal, I just got this job, and I have to tell Lori that in three months I'll be leaving. This is the first job I've ever had, and now I have to give it up."

Sadness filled her young heart as she mourned over the fact that she would soon be leaving and moving to another city.

"But why? Why are you leaving and giving up on this job? Please don't tell me you're quitting? It's been tough and I know Vickie's been getting on your nerves. Heck, she gets on mine, too, but I get through it and handle it. Yes, she's slow, lazy and barely does a thing, but Sasha, you can't just leave me here with her. You and I work so well together, and you break down shipment quickly as a team. If you leave, I'll probably get stuck working with her by myself. It'll slow things down and that's not going to be fun at all! I wish they'd just fire her and get it over with! Why are you leaving, Sasha? Is it really that bad to cope with her?"

"Krystal, believe me, it's not because of her and it's not because I want to. Really - it's not about lazy Vickie."

"Well what is it?"

Sucking her teeth, Sasha said, "It's my mom. She got a promotion on her job and is transferring us to Powder Springs, Georgia. I don't want to leave. It sucks, but I have to go."

"Sasha!"

"I know...I know, Krystal!"

With sad face, Krystal asked, "Well where is this Powder Springs place at?"

"It's somewhere outside of Atlanta."

Krystal cocked her head and excitedly said, "Atlanta! Atlanta, Georgia! Wow! I've always wanted to go to there. I've heard so many neat things about it. My mom has this radio station app on her phone, and she listens to music from Atlanta all the time, even in the car. That music is dope, Sasha. I wish I could go. Can I come visit you?"

Sasha was surprised that her friend, Krystal was no longer somber, but was now acting happy and excited for her. Krystal's new demeanor perked her up and helped bring Sasha out of her feeling of sadness.

Without hesitation she answer, "Yeah, sure. Why not! And you know what? I just found out that I get to go to Georgia Tech...for free! I don't have to pay a thing!"

"What! Are you serious? Sasha, you don't know how lucky you are! I wish I could go, too!"

"Really? I guess I am lucky. No, the word is blessed. Mom said it's a blessing from the Lord and that we should be grateful and give thanks to Him for opening this avenue of progression."

Drawing closer to Sasha, Krystal softly said, "Sasha, I hate to say it, but your mom is right. My mom is struggling trying to save money for me through some college fund at her job. I hate seeing how hard she's working just to make sure I can go. That's why I'm here working as many hours as I can get. You're really blessed. Let's just make sure we call each other every day. I'm going to make sure that in two years when I start putting in college applications, that Georgia Tech is my top priority."

"Really? That'll be so awesome, Krystal! The two of us will rule on that campus! Oh yes, we will!"

"Pinkie swear?" Krystal said as she held out her hand to Sasha.

"Yes...pinkie swear," Sasha confidently said.

"Okay, Krystal, we'd best get back to work before Lori gets in. I'll be in the back breaking down the new shipment. If it gets busy out here, just come and get me."

"Oh, and Sasha, if you see any cute shoes back there, please put a pair to the side for me. You know my size."

"Okay. Call me if you need me."

Walking into the stockroom, Sasha smiled and said to herself, "Maybe things won't be so bad after all. Thank you, God."

Chapter 31

"Aunt Cora, do you have time to talk?"

"Sage, honey, can it wait a minute? I was just about to put another lemon pound cake in the oven. The church is having a country bake sale, and I need to make sure that each one is perfect."

"Sure, Aunt Cora. I'll wait, just as long as you remember to bring a large chunk back home for me."

"We shall see, but I really doubt it, Son. My cakes usually don't last that long, but we'll see. You can lick the bowl, if you'd like."

"I think I'll pass on that one."

"Oh, now you're too grown for licking the drippings? I understand. No longer the child, but now a man who desires the real thing."

Sage was the only child of Walter and Dr. Melanie Linendoll of Springfield, Illinois. In childhood, he had gone through and seen the worst tragedy of his young life. At the age of 10, he lost both his parents to a fatal car accident. He actually saw the mangled car, wrapped around a utility pole, from the school bus in which he was riding on a cool spring day. At the time, he was not aware that it was his parents' car that was covered with tarp and surrounded by police and paramedics. As the bus drove past the police-barricaded car, the school children rushed to windows to see what they could of the unfolding drama. The police stopped traffic that day for an accident caused by a drunken driver who ran a stoplight. Unbeknownst to Sage, he was watching the end of an event that would affect him for the rest of his life.

When he returned home from school that day, the neighbor next door was waiting for him in her doorway, with tear-stained eyes, which was the culmination of a day filled with mourning for the loss of her friends. For over 12 years, she had grown to love her next door neighbors and even participated in the birth of Sage.

Bethany Willsworth, a true neighborly friend, was a frequent visitor in their welcoming home. On more than one occasion, she sat at the dinner table and broke bread with the Linendoll family.

The day that Sage stepped off the bus and walked up to her, she was like a stranger to him. Her demeanor was at first frightening to Sage. He wasn't used to seeing Mrs.

Willsworth in this present condition. Her normally happy outlook was missing. There was no joy in her eyes, and her greeting was not the usual expressive banter. He sensed something was wrong as she took his hand and led him into her home.

"Ms. Bethany, what's wrong? Your eyes are red. Don't you feel well?"

"Oh, Sage, it's just an allergy. You have to wait here until someone comes to get you."

"Okay," he said, but wasn't convinced that all was well.

"I'll fix you something to eat while you do your homework, okay?"

She fed him a dinner of meatloaf and mashed potatoes while he waited. No television was turned on that afternoon. No small talk - homework was the priority.

Finally, it was Aunt Cora who came to the door that evening. Giving him a huge hug, she gently explained to Sage what happened and that he would no longer be seeing his mom and dad because they were now in heaven with God and the angels. Aunt Cora and Sage both cried and cried that evening as he lay upon her lap and cried himself to sleep in the warmth of her comforting bosom.

The house where he played ball with his dad, was a place where Christian values were taught and where he also learned how to excel in all he did. The house was put up for sale. It sold quickly. The money was put into a trust fund along with a hefty amount of money from insurance policies, stocks, bonds and investments. Sage's parents had ensured that their child's future would always be financially secure. At the age of ten, he would know nothing of his wealthyinheritance.

Home had been a place of love and strict discipline. It hurt Sage deeply to leave a home where so many wonderful memories had been created and nurtured. Along with having to deal with the pain and grief of losing both of his parents, his packing and moving to Maryland with his aunt, would become a traumatic experience. He loved his aunt -- his mother's baby sister -- but could not get his head wrapped around the idea of leaving his mom and dad in Springfield to start a new life in Baltimore.

His parents were practical people who always believed in saving and preparing for the future. Therefore, they had pre-paid the cemetery years prior to their deaths. Seeing their caskets being encased in a tomb at Roseland Memorial Park did not help. He was not ready for this vision to be ingrained in his young mind. His aunt regretted putting him through the agony of the ritual that caused his small frame to collapse to the ground. All communication with him shut down that day. He would not speak to her or to anyone else for months.

It took months of grief counseling before Sage was able to speak freely again. His appetite became better. He could also sleep without the nightmares. The voices of children in the school bus watching the burgundy-colored car covered with tarp, had finally subsided from his dreams and consciousness. He also stopped dreaming of the creme colored caskets being transported into the tomb.

Aunt Cora saved his life. She greatly resembled his mother and had a voice just as soft and sweet. Cora became his mother and made him feel comfortable in her home in Baltimore, Maryland. Today, he wanted her to be the very first person to see the ring he'd purchased for Jalena.

With the cake set in the oven, she walked into the dining room and kissed Sage on his cheek. Sitting with her, brought back memories of his mom and how she would sit down and look him straight into his eyes when he talked with her. She never let anything distract or draw her away when it came to her baby, Sage. He had her full attention in whatever he needed to say. She listened first - waited and then spoke. Aunt Cora was just like her. It was something that his mother's family had been taught as children growing up in the Bergman household. Their parents demanded this action to always bear witness that they were listening and were interested in what each other had to say. Every word that was said was held in high esteem and accepted as a matter of importance.

So Aunt Cora was now ready to listen to Sage. "Okay, the cake is in the oven and the timer has been set," she said as she sat there next to him.

"I have something I'd like to show you," he nervously said. He then pulled the small bag from his pocket and set it on the table directly in front of his aunt.

"Aunt Cora, before you open it, I need to tell you something."

Placing her hands upon his, she said, "Sage, you don't have to say a thing. I see the logo on the bag. I know what it is, and I'm so happy for the two of you. I just need to ask if you're sure about this. Are you indeed ready to make such a great commitment? It's a huge responsibility."

"Aunt Cora, I love her so much, and I want her in my life permanently. I know it's a cliché, but she is truly the love of my life. I'm consumed with thoughts of her. Not an hour in the day goes by when I am not thinking about Jalena and our future. Everything's planned out. I'm going to take care of her. She's my queen and I want her to be my wife and to be happy. I've already talked with her mom, and she's given her blessing. She's very happy about our impending union."

With tears in her eyes, Aunt Cora said, "Sage, my son, I am beyond proud of you and in what you've become. Soon you'll be a doctor of medicine and a husband to a beautiful woman. I'm happy for you and want you to have some real peace and happiness in your life. I love Jalena, too. She's such a beautiful person inside and out. I know the two of you will be very happy, and that's all I want for you: happiness. You've gone through significant trauma in your life, and it's about time you've gotten some reward for all you've been through. Your mom and dad would be elated by the way you've grown and taken hold of this life. I'm proud of you, and know that they're proud too, Dr. Linendoll. Now, let's see that ring."

Chapter 32

"Okay, Sasha, I'm really tired. It's been a long day, and I need to hang up this phone. I'll talk with you sometime tomorrow. You just remember what I said: Think of it as an adventure. It'll be fun. You mark my words, okay?"

"I will, Cousin J. Love ya."

"Love you too, Sasha. Be good."

"I will. Goodnight."

"Goodnight, love."

Jalena conversed with Sasha and was able to calm her fears. They even talked about making arrangements with Aunt Jessie to have Sasha come back for summer visits when school wasn't in session. Sasha finally understood the importance of this move and how it would impact her future. Sasha was now excited about it.

Laying in the coziness of her bed, Jalena relaxed and thought about the next chapter of her life. It was celebration time -- her birthday. Excitement embraced her as she thought about it.

In just one day I'll be 23 years old. Sure hope Mom makes that Coconut Confetti Cake with butter crème frosting for me. I can taste it right now. Mmm, mmm, mmm. I don't need any other gifts...just that cake with butter pecan ice cream and me sitting in front of a good movie will satisfy everything I need.

This year also marked the second anniversary of her being totally drug free and home again. Healed from the hurt and pain of her sinful past, she was now headed for greatness. She didn't like thinking about the past, but thoughts about it and everything she put her family through, especially her mom, would pop up in her mind every now and then.

Terrible things happened that she was still ashamed of. The drinking and drugs caused her family much hurt. Jalena's bragging caused gang members to break into the house, rob it and hurt her mom. The memories of her destructive behavior saddened Jalena when thinking back on the past.

Tears filled her eyes. Praying she said, "Thank you, God. Jared got here just in time. Jared was a hero that day and I was the enemy, thrown out of the house by my family. It's a time that I'd like to erase from my memory, but I just can't. What if mom hadn't forgiven me? Where would I be today? So I thank and praise you Lord God. You are the giver and restorer of life."

Jalena digressed even more into her thoughts as she remembered the day she walked up to the house and her mother opened the door. Words of apology and regret flowed from her lips as she pleaded for forgiveness. In her mind, she saw herself standing there face to face, hungering for her mother's forgiveness and unconditional love.

The memory of all that happened was a catalyst in keeping her rooted and grounded. She never wanted to make the same mistakes. What a lesson learned. The past was no longer being held against Jalena. Forgiveness was her great healer.

Life was good. She had a good man, a good job, family and friends surrounding her and the peace of God. Jalena was in a place of serenity, and excited about the next chapter of life.

For her birthday, she wanted nothing more than to celebrate with family and friends. Sage would definitely be a part of this scenario. He'd already made plans to take her out for dinner but wouldn't tell her where they were going. Jalena was excited about spending time with

him, but didn't want to leave her family out of the celebration.

Although tired, she opened her bible, read a Scripture
and prayed.

"Father God, I bless you and thank you for this wonderful day. You kept me from all hurt, harm and danger
and I —"

With the heaviness of her eyelids taking control, she
drifted off to sleep before ending her prayer. Falling
quickly into a deep sleep, she was once again dancing in
the arms of God, in the same place and dressed in a white
empire dress with a red ribbon floating in the air.

"Hello, Jalena." A multitude of angels were all
around, welcoming her with open, fluttering wings. They
were round about her and God as she danced with him
to a minuet. God spoke and it was as if there were no
breaks in their previous conversation.

"Welcome, my child - welcome back. I just wanted to
tell you how grateful I am to you for taking the time with
Delia. I'm so proud of you and how you helped to lead
her back to Me by ministering to her each day. You are a
great example of how easy it is for broken vessels to be
remolded and reshaped into vessels of honor that can be
used for My glory. This is your season, and you are a true
treasure."

Jalena wasn't able to respond. Words could not express how she was feeling. Angels played on harps, while others fluttered their wings saturating the air with the pleasant fragrance of roses. She continued her dancing in the heavens as God said,

"You'll be happy to know that Delia and I had a long talk. I personally danced her into heaven. Thank you, Jalena, for your labor - it was not in vain. I have so much more in store because of the obedience you've shown. Continue in My way and blessings will overtake you."

These were the last words Jalena heard as she felt movement on her lap.

"Oh, I'm sorry, I didn't mean to wake you," Marinda said as she remove the Bible from Jalena's lap and placed it on the nightstand.

"I peeked in and saw that you were asleep. I just wanted to make sure that you were warm enough. You know how chilly it gets in here during the night."

"That's okay, Mom, even though I was having a beautiful dream."

"Really? What was it about?"

Not really wanting to say too much more, Jalena groggily said, "Can I tell you some other time? I'm really tired and have a long day tomorrow."

Marinda covered Jalena and gave her a kiss on the forehead. "Goodnight, baby girl. I love you."

"Love you more, Mom." The light was turned off and the door shut. Tears began flowing as Jalena remembered His words. Those words brought comfort to the very depths of her soul. She felt honored that God was pleased and said she was a treasure. Tearfully she whispered, "No one's ever called me a treasure before...no one."

Hoping to fall back into the arms of God, she closed her eyes. She peacefully slept - no more dreams.

Chapter 33

A new day quickly dawned, and the entire household was up and already engaged in preparing for the day's activities. Marinda was in the kitchen, frying some bacon for Jared who was in the shower. She also made bag lunches for each of her children. Jalena overslept. She was now rushing trying to get out the door and grabbed her lunch, while kissing her mom on the cheek.

"Thanks, Mom," she said, as she headed towards the door.

"Why are you rushing out, Jalena?"

"I'm trying to catch the 7:45 Metro, Mom."

"Don't worry about that today. Sage is outside waiting on you. He also stopped at Starbucks and got you a danish and some green tea. He just got here."

"Really? Well thank you, Jesus. I won't be late. I'm perspiring already trying to get to work. See you later, Mom. Love ya!"

"Love ya more."

Marinda continued cooking and preparing a small breakfast for herself and Jared who was now making his way down the stairs.

"Jared, you know tomorrow is your sister's birthday, right?"

"Yes, Mom, I know."

"What are you getting her? I hope you're getting her something special. Right?"

"Okay, Mom. I know you're fishing for an answer."

"Since you already know, then tell me what your plans are for your sister."

Jared hesitated, blessed his food and picked up a slice of bacon from his plate and chewed slowly.

Popping him in the head, Marinda said, "Boy, if you don't tell me right now, you're gonna get—"

"All right, all right, Mom."

He finished chewing, swallowed and then slowly said. "You know that old car Dad had? The ancient Jaguar that wasn't working and you told me to get rid of it? Well - I didn't. A few of the guys and I have been working hard on it for months. We put in a new engine, new plugs, tire rod, brakes, brand new tires, water pump, exhaust and upholstery. Everything is new inside and out. Even had it painted deep blue. Mom, I tell you, that car is hot, and she's gonna love it! Almost tried to keep it for myself."

She was speechless. Marinda couldn't believe what she was hearing. This news gave her an unspeakable joy. Her son had saved the car. It was something she wanted most. Although she told him to get rid of it, she was hoping he would ignore her. Words couldn't express how deeply she was feeling within. She walked around the counter and gave Jared the biggest hug and kiss.

Marinda didn't have to say a word. Jared knew what his mother was feeling. He felt much pride and joy when the job was completed at the shop. He tried to man up, holding back his own tears. He didn't want to show any kind of emotion as he kissed Marinda on the cheek and jumped up as if now in a rush to get out to work.

That car meant a lot to his dad, and everyone knew it. He purchased the automobile at an auction and was never able to get it working properly. Eventually he gave up and covered it with a tarp. Jared's conscience would not allow him to get rid of the old car. When his dad died he had it towed to the garage where it rested from that time on.

Many late night hours were spent working to repair the Jaguar. It was now ready for presentation as a classy, beautiful piece of workmanship - finally finished and ready to be handed over to his sister for her birthday celebration. This was going to be very emotional for Jalena - a gift she'd always embrace for the memories of her dad and for the love it took in bringing it to life.

Chapter 34

J alena made it to work in plenty of time. As she entered into the office, she saw a beautiful crystal vase filled with thorn-less red roses sitting on her desk. These beautiful flowers have to be from my Sage, she thought as she placed her purse and lunch in the desk drawer. Sitting, Jalena removed the card attached to the vase and read the message.

My love, I know your birthday is not until tomorrow, but I couldn't wait to tell you how much I love you by sending you these red roses. You, Jalena Mathesin, are the love of my life, the apple of my eye. You are my reason for waking up each morning. Just knowing that I will either see you or hear your sweet voice makes my heart skip a beat. I love you so very much and will love you for the rest of my days. Love you much, Sage.

Even with this note filled with a lot of clichés, a lump formed in her throat. Jalena wanted to cry as she read his lovely words. She felt his heart in every single word. Jalena had a hard time composing herself as she took the card with both hands and held it to her heart. She was touched just knowing how much he really loved her. This would indeed be a beautiful day.

At that moment, Laurie walked in.

"Hi, Jalena."

"Hey, Laurie. You good?"

"I'm fine. Just a little tired, had a late night. Oh, what beautiful roses!" Laurie said as she approached Jalena's desk. Leaning over to smell them she asked, "Are they from Sage?"

"Now, Laurie, who else would be sending me roses like these?"

"I don't know. Mr. Peters, perhaps?"

"Seriously? You've got to be kidding."

"Jalena, there's been a rumor spreading for a few months now. He's been acting like he has a real crush on you."

"Please, Laurie. That's totally ridiculous and don't go around repeating that lie. There's only one man in my life and that's the one and only Sage Linendoll."

With a smirk, Laurie said, "You mind if I read the card?"

"Yes, I do mind. This card is for my eyes alone," said Jalena as she put the card into her purse.

"So, Jalena, what's the occasion? Why's he sending you red roses? You do know that red roses mean romantic love and thorn-less means love at first sight. What's going on?"

"Well, tomorrow, I'll be celebrating my twenty-third birthday."

"Really? And he's sending you red roses? Why didn't you tell anyone it's your birthday, especially me? I would have gotten you a card - maybe even a gift?"

As Laurie spoke, Mr. Peters walked into the office holding onto a long, purple and silver gift wrapped box.

"Happy birthday, Jalena," he said as he handed it to her.

Hesitation embraced Jalena and she said, "Oh...thank you...Mr. Peters. How nice of you." She wasn't quite sure what to make of this gesture as He placed the box into her hand.

"I know you're celebrating your birthday tomorrow, and the partners and I just wanted to thank you for all of your hard work this past year. You've been very instrumental in helping us get a lot of contracts out on time, and our clients have been pleased with the work. So thank you and have a happy birthday. Before I forget, Laurie, Mr. Jacobs would like to see you in his office."

"Oh...Okay, I'll head over right away." Laurie gathered her notepad and pen and left the office.

When she was out of sight, he sat down on the corner of Jalena's desk and said, "Well aren't you going to open it?"

Looking at the box, Jalena said, "I think I'll wait until tomorrow to open it with my other birthday gifts."

"Oh," he said with a glint of obvious frustration.

Seeing his facial expression, Jalena said, "But if you'd like me to, I'll open it right now."

So she picked up the box and carefully tore away the gift wrap. When she saw the logo for Jared® The Galleria Of Jewelry, she suddenly stopped removing the shiny silver.

"You know, Jalena, this gift is actually from me," he proudly said.

Looking up at him, she sarcastically said, "Oh, so you went to Jared®."

"Yes, I did. You know, I've had my eyes on you for some time and –"

"No, I didn't know," Jalena said with disdain. This had no affect on him. He continued his speech with boldness.

"I was wondering if you'd be interested in having lunch or dinner with me sometime this coming week."

"Well, I –"

Before Jalena could fully respond, Laurie returned to the office, talking on her Bluetooth as she sat down at her computer. Feeling somewhat uncomfortable and irritated that she had been placed in this awkward position, Jalena looked at him and brusquely said, "Mr. Peters, is there anything else I can help you with?"

"No, but we'll continue our conversation later," he said with a quick wink of the eye.

She sat there stunned and outdone that He didn't get the hint of her disinterest in him. He acted as if everything was copacetic. Jalena didn't know what to make of him or of this proposition. She was shocked and pushed his gift to the side of the desk, not daring to even completely open the box.

Finished with her call, Laurie asked, "What did they give you?"

Jalena was too embarrassed to answer and didn't want to let Laurie know or give her any indication of what had actually just taken place.

She tried her best to sound cheerful and said, "Oh, I started to open it but decided to wait until my actual birthday on tomorrow."

"Okay...I guess I'll have to wait and see. For my birthday, they gave me a nice pen set. That's probably what you've been given, too."

Jalena placed the box in her desk. She was anxious to get away from the troubling conversation and said, "Let me get to work. I've got a lot to do before the end of day. I'm sure you do, too, Laurie."

"Yes, I do, Mr. Jacobs just gave me a big project for a new contract. It has to be completed by next Thursday evening."

"Okay, well let's get it done," said Jalena.

She tried hard to concentrate on work but was distracted by what had transpired. She then decided to put the gift into her purse, not wanting to leave it there during the weekend. Her mind was now filled with confusion. How am I going to handle this? This can't happen, not now! Didn't he even see these flowers from Sage on my desk? Oh my God, please give me a way out of this crappie mess!!

Chapter 35

"Jalena, Jalena. Birthday girl, it's time to wake up! Get up, baby girl! It's your birthday!" Marinda was at the head of Jalena's bed with a tray. The smell of bacon, cheese eggs and baked rolls should have been enough to awaken her, but the stress of the previous day's event caused her difficulties in sleeping. She finally drifted off in the early morning hours. Being gracious and happy about this wakeup call was hard to display.

"Mom, thank you, but you really didn't have to do any of this."

"Oh, yes, I did. Today is your special day. Before you get up and out of here with Sage, I want us to celebrate together. Family will be here tonight, but this is our time...yours and mine. Now sit up and give me room to set up your tray."

"Okay, okay, Mom." Jalena took a moment and rubbed her eyes to wake up and focus. After setting the tray on the bedside table, Marinda helped arrange the pillows behind Jalena's back and neck as she sat up.

Marinda beamed with pride as she picked up the tray and placed it carefully in front of Jalena.

"This looks so good, Mom. Are these fresh-baked rolls?"

"Yes, they are. Just for you."

"Mmm...mmm..mmm...Thanks, Mom."

On the edge of the tray was a small, gift-wrapped box. "Open the box, please," Marinda excitedly said.

As Jalena picked up the box, her mind took a sudden detour to opening the box from Mr. Peters. Shaking herself from that memory, she opened her Mom's gift.

"Aww..." Jalena smiled.It was a mother/daughter necklace.

"Oh, Mom, this is beautiful! I love it!"

"I'm glad you like it. I wanted to get something special that we both can share. We've been through so much together. I thank God that He worked things out the way He did. You know, December will be the second anniversary of your coming home and being drug free."

"Yes, I'm happy about that! When I was out there, I never thought this day would ever be in the picture.

Mom, thank you so much for taking me back in and forgiving me. I know you didn't have to."

"Jalena, I forgave you the day you were put out of this house. Tough love was needed to get you to the point of knowing how serious the situation was. You would either die out there, or God was going to bring you back to me delivered. I had to make that decision based on those two things. Every day I prayed for you, I knew that someway...somehow, you would come back home different and God answered my prayers."

All Jalena could do was smile as she listened to her mom. Reaching into the box, she bent the heart into two at the perforation.

"Here, Mom, let me help you put yours on first and then you put mine around my neck."

It was very ceremonious as mother and daughter exchanged the pieces of the heart. At that moment, they knew that their love was bonded together and nothing could ever come between or separate what they shared. Wiping away tears, they embraced each other. Nothing else was said. Marinda left Jalena to enjoy her birthday breakfast in bed.

Chapter 36

J alena decided to put the scene with Mr. Peters out of her mind. She refused to let it distract her today of all days. Her birthday was going to be a phenomenal day with family and friends. Sage was taking her out for dinner, and Marinda made plans for a family party to take place that evening. She was excited! This was going to be a great day.

Tahlia was meeting her at the mall for lunch. Afterwards, they were going to pick out something extra special to wear for the birthday celebration.

Rushing down the stairs she yelled, "Jared, I'm ready!"

"Ready for what, may I ask?"

"Please, Jared...not today. Please, not today! Remember, you said you would drop me off at Harborplace. I'm meeting Tahlia there. Don't worry about picking me up. She'll give me a ride home."

"I know, I know. I'm just messing with you. Happy Birthday, Sis," he said and then hugged her tightly.

Trying to rush him out the door, Jalena said, "Thank you, Jared. Now come on, let's go! I'll see you later, Mom!"

Marinda caught Jalena's arm before she was able to get out the door and said, "Jalena, don't be too late getting back. What time is Sage picking you up for dinner?"

"Oh, he said between 6 and 6:30. I'll be back way before that time. Don't worry, Mom. Everything has to be just right for tonight, and I need plenty of time to get myself together. Love you!"

"Love you more!"

Jared and Jalena headed outside. In the driveway sat a beautiful car, all shiny and new.

"Wow! Jared, whose car is this sitting in our driveway? It's a beauty. I wonder who it belongs to?"

Pensively, Jared said, "I'm not sure. Let's go and check it out."

Walking down the stairs and across the lawn, they made their way over to the car. Marinda stood back on the stairs watching and getting emotional.

"Let's take a closer look," said Jared. Hmm...look at this. There's a name inscribed in small, gold scripted letters right here below the driver-side mirror.

Jalena looked closely and for a moment, didn't say a word. When it finally dawned upon her what was happening, she screamed, "No! No! This can't be! It's mine? Jared, it's mine?"

"Yes, Sis, it's yours. All yours. Happy Birthday, J!"

"Are you serious? I can't believe this. It's mine, all mine."

Jared then asked her a question that caught Jalena off guard. "Does it look familiar in any way to you?"

She took a closer look at the outside features and softly said, "It's Daddy's car. The one he was trying to fix, isn't it?"

Overcome with emotion, Jalena felt her knees weaken and slumped to the ground, crying like a baby. Marinda ran out to join them. She and Jared sat with Jalena, comforting her as she cried tears of joy. Admiring the workmanship, Jared explained what took place to restore the old car.

This was the missing link of a jigsaw. It was the final piece needed to help Jalena fully heal. She was now free from feeling the burden of guilt she had long been holding on to. Not being with her dad when he took his last breath was a condemnation she couldn't let go of. The receipt of this gift meant so much to her. She felt it was a birthday gift sent from heaven above from her dad. This was significant. She was still his baby girl and she could feel his presence as her Mom and Jared embraced her, releasing tears of joy and happiness. Her real breakthrough had come.

Chapter 37

J alena was on her way to meet Tahlia. Marinda was back in the kitchen preparing for the party. She had a lot of cooking to do in preparation for the big event.

Jared returned from the market picking up a few last minute items and entering the house, he said, "Mom, guess who I found coming up the driveway?"

"Who?"

"It's me, Momma Marinda. Sage."

"Sage! How are you, Son?"

"I'm good. Just a little nervous."

Marinda hugged him and said, "Today is a big day, huh? I am so excited!"

"Yes, it is. I sent Jalena a dozen red roses to her job. I hope she liked them. I haven't heard anything from her since I saw her yesterday morning."

"Oh, she loves them. She has them on the mantelpiece in her room and wanted to wait until today to thank you. She said there'd be a great big, juicy kiss just for you."

Jared screwed up his face and said, "Mom, that sounds so gross."

"Just mind your business, Jared. Well, Sage, today is her birthday, and I have a feeling this is the day you and I talked about on the way from the airport. Am I correct in that assumption?"

"Yes, ma'am. This is the day. I knew you'd be celebrating her birthday with family, so I figured I'd somehow fit it in with the festivities."

Marinda had a great big grin on her face.

Jared began to get curious and said, "Will someone please let me in on what's going on besides Jalena's birthday party? Something else is happening. What is it?"

Sage reached into his jacket and pulled out a small, blue-velvet box and said, "I wanted to get here and show it to you, Momma Marinda. I hope it meets with your approval." Carefully, he opened the box and showed it to both Marinda and Jared.

"Wow!" said Jared. "That's some rock -- an engagement ring. That's beautiful. She's going to love it."

Marinda didn't say a word, but tears began streaming down her face.

Sensing his mom was weeping, Jared stood behind her and wrapped his arms around her, saying, "That's okay, Mom. I know what you're thinking. It's okay to cry. Your baby girl and my 'big Sis,' all grown up and getting married. It's okay, Mom."

Choking back his own tears he said, "Sage, you did good, Bruh...you did good. Welcome to the family." He then reached out and shook Sages hand.

Holding tight to Jared's hand he said, "I love Jalena so much. I don't want either of you to ever worry about her or doubt me. She'll be well taken care of, and I will be a good husband to her and father for our children."

"Grandchildren!" shouted Miranda with joy. "Oh, I just can't wait!"

Letting go of Jared's hand he said, "Now that won't be right away. It's something Jalena and I will discuss at some point, but not too soon."

As Marinda was wiping away her tears she said, "Sage, I trust you to do everything you've said, but let me tell you a few things."

Jared interrupted and said. "Okay, man, get ready for your sermon."

Marinda slapped Jared on the arm and said, "You can learn a few things too! So as I was saying before I was so rudely interrupted - Sage, be the man of your household, a man of wisdom and valor. Go to church as a family.

You lead the way. Spend time reading God's word and go on vacations together. Don't ever depend on your wife to bring in the household income. If she wants to work, let her work. If she'd rather be a housewife taking care of the home, let her do that. Don't you ever get so caught up in your job that you forget about your family. Raise your children united as one, bonded together with one voice. Don't put any constraints on each other; it takes away the enjoyment. Communication is valuable. Talk, don't yell to fix your disagreements and never lay a hand on her. If you get angry, take that anger out the door until you can cool off and never go to bed angry with each other."

"Wow, Mom," said Jared. "You just said a mouthful in one breath! And let me add something. Sage, things get hard...arguments happen, but if you ever lay a finger on my sister, that'll be the first and last time. If you ever do anything to hurt her or if I even see an unusual mark on her, I'll—"

"Jared, come on, man. That'll never happen. Please believe me. Jalena is my queen and that's the way she'll be treated. Don't worry."

"I know, but it's just a little warning, Sir."

Smiling, Marinda said, "Okay, you two, that's enough. I have a lot to do before tonight. I still have to bake the cake and get things straightened out before everyone gets here. Jared, you know what you have to do, so get on with it, Son."

"Right away, Mom."

Sage asked, "Is there anything I can do to help, Momma Marinda?"

"Yes, there is one thing you can do starting now. I know that I can't ever replace your own mom, nor am I trying to, so the one thing you can do that would make me happy is for you to just call me Mom. Not Momma Marinda, but Mom, if that's okay with you."

"Nothing would make me happier, Mom."

"Thank you, Son. Now you get going and do whatever you have to do to prepare yourself for this evening...love you."

"Love you, too, Mom."

Chapter 38

J alena made it to the mall and from the parking lot shouted, "Tahlia! Tahlia! Can't she see me?" Okay, finally got her attention. It's going to be so much fun spending time with her."

After losing Trisha, Tahlia stepped right in and made things easier for Jalena to handle. She helped her to get over the sadness and loneliness Jalena was really feeling with the loss of her friend. She couldn't take Trisha's place, but did a great job at being that friend Jalena was in need of.

"Tahlia!"

"Jalena! Hey, birthday girl. Happy Birthday to you," she said in a sing song voice. "Girl, let me give you a hug."

"Thank you! Thank you!" Jalena said with a slight curtsy.

"Let me give you this birthday card now. There's a mall gift card in it that you can use right here."

"Tahlia, thank you so much! I'll use this today!"

"That's the plan, my sister!"

"Lunch first or shopping?" Jalena asked.

"Jalena, I believe we better shop first. If we eat first, I don't know about you, but that demon of tiredness will come on me so quick, I won't be able to do a thing but sleep walk. Believe me, it's not something you want to see live and in color. Not too pretty."

"You're right. Let's get going! Teabots, here we come!"

The two of them walked the entire mall, buying dresses, shoes and other sale items. Jalena was even able to pick up that red maxi cardigan she'd been eyeing for several weeks. This time, she caught it on sale.

Worn out, they made their way to the restaurant for lunch. As they arrived, Jalena couldn't wait to sit down. "My feet are burning and cursing at me. I have to get in there and take these things off! I should've worn something more comfortable."

"Jalena, what did I tell you the other day when we were making plans for today?"

Jalena smirking said, "Um..."

"You know what I said. Don't play ignorant now. I told you to wear sneakers, but you insist on trying to look cute all the time wearing pumps. It serves you right."

"Is that anyway for you to talk, Evangelist?"

"Just trying to bring a wise word of correction and wisdom: Wear comfort shoes when you shop, Girlfriend," she said laughing.

Walking up to them, the hostess said, "Good afternoon, ladies. Welcome to the Angelcake Factory. Seating for two?"

"Yes, a booth please," Tahlia said."

They placed their packages into the booth first. Jalena quickly removed her shoes and breathed a big sigh of relief.

"Whew...the pain...oh the pain...mmm...mmm...mmm. That feels a lot better."

"All right now, you better be careful about that. My momma always says that when you walk around in tight shoes, your feet swell when you take them off. Hope you'll be able to get them back on. It's a long walk back to the entrance we came in."

"Being the good friend that you are and since you have your comfort shoes on, I'm so sure you wouldn't mind going to get the car and bringing it to this entrance. Am I not right? I don't mind waiting. I'll hold your bags for you. Oh, but wait, wait just one little, bitty minute. Guess what?"

"What?"

"I'm no longer in need of a ride home...no bus and no more cabs," Jalena proudly said.

"And why not? Is Jared coming to get you?"

"No, ma'am, I'm now the owner of my own car! A beautiful car! Tahlia, you have to see it," she said with excitement.

"Really, Jalena?"

"Yes!"

"I'm so happy for you! That's terrific! Tell me about it! When and where did you get it?"

"Well, do you remember that old car my dad had in the garage? The one that he was working on for the longest time and never got it to start up?"

"No! Are you serious? You're not driving around in that old piece of junk, are you?"

"Tahlia, girl, when you see it, you're going to be shocked. It's not the same car you remember. Emma has had her own Cinderella story -- a true makeover -- wait till you see her."

"Oh, now she has a name? Jalena, you oughta quit."

"I'm serious, Tahlia. Jared restored her, and she looks brand new. I'm telling you. I was shocked when I realized what he had done. I thought he'd dumped the car. Do you know how it makes me feel to be driving around in that car? Driving here, I couldn't help but think about the time and energy that Dad spent trying to fix that old car. It's like new now. It's made me appreciate my brother even more for taking the time to fix it up for me."

"Wow, Jalena. That's great! Now that's a gift from God!"

"Yes, it's a gift - my special gift straight from heaven given from my daddy. The seats are reupholstered and everything's new. It's just like a brand-new vehicle and has that new car smell. It's like a having a gift personally gift wrapped and hand delivered from heaven. It makes me feel so good deep inside. Ooh...I'm sorry; I get choked up just thinking about it."

"That's okay, Sis. Cry if you have to. That's the best birthday gift ever."

"Yes! It is."

Looking at the time, Tahlia said, "Now we'd better get moving. I've got a quick meeting at 4 o'clock with the choir today. What are you ordering?"

"I'm eating light. Sage is taking me out to dinner tonight."

"Where to?"

"Crazy guy won't tell me, but I'm hoping it's someplace romantic and cozy...not a diner."

"You really love that man, don't you?"

"Yes, I do," she said with a big grin.

The waitress came to their table. "Hello, ladies. My name is Sarah. I'll be your server today. Are you ready to order?"

"Hi, Sarah," they said in unison.

"First, what would you like to drink?"

"I'll have water with lemon," Tahlia said.

"The same for me with a few extra lemons on the side, and can we order now?"

"Jalena!"

"Well, aren't you hungry? I am!"

"Yes, I can take your orders now."

"Sweet! I'll have the small turkey wrap and garden salad with French dressing. Just a tiny bit of onions on the salad, please. Gotta keep the breath fresh and that's it," Jalena said happily.

"And I'll have the lunch salmon with all the trimmings, please. Thank you, Sarah," said Tahlia.

"Thank you, ladies. I'll be right back with your orders."

As the waitress walked away, Jalena reached in her purse, found what she was looking for and handed it to Tahlia. "Look at this," she said.

Opening the plastic bag, Tahlia pulled out the purple and silver box. "Oh, thank you, Jalena, but you didn't have to get me a gift. It's your birthday today, not mine."

"It's not for you, silly. It was given to me yesterday, and I was afraid to open it."

"Now why on earth would you be afraid to open a gift? Listen, you and I have been friends for a long time. If I don't know anything else about you, the one thing I do know is that you love receiving gifts. So, my dear, why would you be afraid to open this gift."

"Open it first, and then I'll tell you."

Tahlia continued tearing the gift wrapping where Jalena had ended. "Mmm...Jared®'s Galleria."

Once the paper was completely removed, she opened the box and said, "Wow!"

"What is it? What is it," Jalena anxiously said. She was now ready for the big reveal.

"See for yourself, Jalena. It's beautiful."

Tahlia carefully handed the gift to Jalena. "A diamond necklace," screamed Jalena.

"Hey! Lower your voice. Did Sage give this to you?"

"No, Tahlia. Mr. Peters gave it to me for my birthday."

The look on Tahlia's face was one of shock. "Jalena...No! You've got to give this back. You can't take a present like this from your boss. He's just not any man. This could really cause you a lot of trouble."

"Don't you think I know this, Tahlia. I've got to give it right back. He gave it to me yesterday and asked me to have dinner or lunch with him."

"What did you say?"

"I didn't get a chance to say anything. Laurie walked back into the office before I could say a word. I had to change the conversation so that she wouldn't suspect anything. You know what a gossipmonger she is."

"Jalena, what're you going to do? What will Sage think? Are you going to tell him?"

"Yes, I'll tell him. I just have to find the right time and words."

"Why is it so hard? Do you have feelings for Mr. Peters?"

"Seriously? Tahlia, I know you didn't just ask me that foolish question. No! I don't have feelings for that man. He's rude and arrogant."

"He's also very rich," said Tahlia.

"So! Then you go after him. Tahlia, I have a man – a good man who loves me, and I love him."

"Jalena, I'm just giving you something to think about. You really don't have any official tie to Sage. There's no ring on your finger. Until that day comes, you are free to do what you want and when you want. You can see any man you want on your own terms."

"Oh, my gosh! I really can't believe you, Tahlia. Here's the deal: Hold onto that necklace for me till Monday. I'll meet you in the concourse to get it around 10am so I can return it to Mr. Peters before lunch. That's all there is to it. I'll tell him I have no interest in dating him when I hand it back over to him."

"Okay...okay, if you say so. I'll be glad to hold onto it, but can I try it on?"

"No, Tahlia! Just leave it in the box. I don't want anything to happen to it. No telling how much he spent on that thing. Do you have money to replace it if it gets lost, stolen or broken? No, you don't. So just put it in your purse and leave it there until Monday. Okay?"

Sighing, Tahlia agreed.

"Here's your lunch, ladies. Enjoy."

Chapter 39

J alena made it home in plenty of time to take a short nap and then prepared for the celebration.

"Jalena, may I come in?"

"Sure, Mom. I'm just getting out of the shower. See the new dress I bought, hanging on the closet door?"

"Yes, that's gorgeous. I love it."

Jalena shouting from the bathroom said, "When I saw it, I fell in love with the royal blue color and the shear, three-quarter length sleeves. It fits me well. Sage is going to love it. I even got black platform pumps that accessorize perfectly."

"Wow! They're so high!"

"Mom, they're not that high compared to some others I have."

"I guess not."

Finally stepping out of the steamy bathroom, Jalena began getting ready. "Can't be late for this date," she said with a smile.

"Are you excited to go out with Sage tonight?" Marinda asked.

"I really am, Mom. This is the first time he's actually taking me to someplace special other than a diner. He hasn't even told me where we're going. I'm excited and can't wait."

"I'm excited, too! When you get back, we'll celebrate even more with family and friends. Do you need help getting ready?"

"No, Mom. I'm good."

"It's 6 o'clock. He's a very timely, so you'd better hurry...chop...chop. Let me know if you need anything."

"Yes, Mom, I will. This night is going to be so special. I can't wait!"

After her mother left the room, Jalena sat down and thought about the beautiful necklace.

It's no longer in my hands; it's out of my sight. Mr. Peters is not going to ruin this night with my man. No way I'll let that happen. Out of sight...out of mind. I just hope Tahlia doesn't try to wear it and she keeps our secret.

Marinda yelled, "Jalena! Hurry! There's a white limo outside!"

Looking out her window and couldn't believe her eyes. "Wow! Sage actually got us a limousine, and it's gold trimmed. I feel special right now. I better hurry up and get ready."

"Jalena, the limousine driver just got out of the car and is opening the door for Sage. He has a single white rose in his hand."

"Mom, what are you doing? Giving a play by play?"

"No, but you better hurry because there's a handsome man walking up the driveway ready for you."

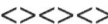

As Sage walked up to the house, his head filled with nervous thoughts. The magnitude of what he was about to do made him jittery.

What should I say and how? More importantly, what will she say? I'm on my way to fulfill a most important part of our destiny. What if she rejects my proposal? Wait a minute! Jalena's my queen, so there's no doubt in my mind what her answer will be. I have plans for her...a future for us. She's going to be just as excited as I am.

Marinda opened the door and said, "Well, don't you look handsome."

Sage was wearing a gray, double-breasted Armani suit.

"Thanks, Mom."

"Looking sharp, Bruh," said Jared.

"Thank you," he said with a twinge of nervousness.

Marinda sensed that Sage was struggling and said, "It'll be just fine. Don't you go worrying. Dispel any fear and go with your heart."

She handed him a cool glass of water and the three of them sat and engaged in small talk as they waited for Jalena to make her grand entrance.

Chapter 40

As she walked down the hallway towards the stairs, Jalena felt like a school girl on her way to meet her prom king. As she approached the head of the stairs, Sage stood. He looked up at her as if it were the very first time he had ever seen her. Jalena felt and looked amazing. Watching him stare at her, she knew that he was awed by her appearance. She felt a little embarrassed by his reaction. He seemed to be in a trance as he watched her descend the staircase. When she got to the bottom landing, he snapped back into a state of reality and said, "My gorgeous, Jalena. You are so beautiful, my love." He then gave her a passionate kiss.

"Come on, you guys, not here," sneered Jared.

Marinda, now in tears as she watched the two of them, said, "Jalena, baby girl, you look so beautiful,"

"Mom, don't cry. We're just going on a date."

"Well, this is the first time I've seen the two of you go out dressed up like this. Wait a minute, let me get my camera."

"Mom!"

"Just hold on."

Marinda grabbed her camera and stood in the corner beaming as she flashed pictures. Her desire for Jalena had finally come to pass. God had answered her prayers by sending her daughter a good man who loved God and loved Jalena.

"Sis, you look hot. If we weren't related, I'd try to take you from Sage myself."

"Hold up, my man, that's not a kosher thing for you to say to your sister and even if that were the case, there'd be no way that I'd let it happen. We'd have to fight to the death for sure."

Breaking up this little confab, Jalena said, "Shouldn't we be leaving? I'm anxious to see what my handsome man has got planned for me this evening," she coyly said.

"Yes, my love. Let us be gone. Your chariot has arrived and awaits you, my queen."

"Geesh," said Jared. "Would you two just leave? You're making me jealous with all of this passion stuff in the air. I need to go out and find me a girl to take off some of this pressure I'm feeling."

"Jared!" Marinda yelled.

"Sorry, Mom, but—"

"But nothing," she laughed."Now you two go and have a nice time. We'll be here waiting for you."

Jalena asked, "With Coconut Confetti Cake, Mom?"

"Yes, Jalena, I'll have your Coconut Confetti Cake with raspberry jam between each layer, topped with butter crème frosting."

"Mmm...mmm...mmm. Wait till you taste it, Sage. It will become one of your favorites, too! See you later. Love you, guys!"

"Love you more," they said in unison.

Marinda watched from the window with Jared as they got into the limo.

"There they go, Mom. Your baby girl will officially be engaged in marriage before the night is over...on her birthday."

"Yes, Son. I'm overwhelmed and happy for her. She deserves this happiness."Sighing, she said, "Now let me go finish that cake."

Chapter 41

J alena felt like royalty as the limousine driver opened the door for her, and Sage took her hand, helping her into the car. This was her first experience ever riding in a limousine. She sat and took in every little detail. A large bottle of non-alcoholic champagne sat in a crystal champagne bucket. It was immersed in small, lilac-colored ice cubes that were shaped like little hearts. There were also two crystal fluted glasses. One glass had Jalena's initial inscribed on it, and the other initialed "S" for Sage. He had really outdone himself for this date.

She could feel Sage watching as she took in every-thing she saw. He then asked, "Are you happy?"

"Sage, what do you think? This is a birthday I'll never forget. We haven't even gotten to dinner yet, and I am both overwhelmed and excited by everything that's already taken place. This is like the prom night I didn't get to attend. Thank you so much."

"No, my love, thank you. You've really turned my tragic life around. For so long, I didn't think that I'd ever be able to love anyone because of the sadness I felt deep within my heart. Losing my parents in that tragic accident left a scab that was hard to heal. No matter how much I tried to get rid of those feelings, nothing helped to unmask my deeply hurt feelings. But then you came along and changed all of that".

"But, Sage—"

"No...please let me finish. Jalena, before God placed you in my life, there were days when I thought I'd die from loneliness and the hurt I was feeling. You came and turned everything around. Even when we were in high school, there were days I wanted to end it all. You came and gave me purpose. It was a struggle, but I made it through prayer and faith that God would one day break the back of demons off of my life. Jalena, you have no idea how much you really mean to me. I can no longer live without you in my life."

"Sage, you—"

"No, baby, please don't say a word. Just listen to me. I know you've also gone through a lot in your life and would probably say the same things about me, but tonight is about you and my expressions of love to you and how much you've affected my life. Girl, I love you so much and only want what's best for you. Every day of my life, without fail, in some way, shape or form, I'm going to show you just how much you mean to me."

Pushing a button directly in front of him, he said, "William, as soon as you can, please pull over?"

"Yes, Sir, Mr. Linendoll."

"I'm sorry, but I just can't wait any longer."

"Sorry about what, Sage," Jalena said concerned.

William, his driver, pulled the limousine over and parked at the nearest corner of the intersection. As soon as the car stopped, the he got out, opened the door and immediately, Sage jumped out of the car.

Jalena couldn't imagine what was happening and said, "Sage, what are you doing?"

"Jalena, I just can't wait."

She pensively said, "Wait for what?"

"For this, baby, for this. Can you step out of the car?"

"I can, but why?" He offered his hand to Jalena, she slid over and took his hand. She carefully stepped out of the limo.

When she was steady on her feet, Sage dropped down on one knee and said, "I love you so much, Jalena Mathesin."

As Sage pulled the blue-velvet box out of his jacket pocket, Jalena then realized what was happening and tears began to fall. People standing around the busy street corner stopped to watch and began pulling out cell phones, taking pictures.

As he took the ring and held it out before her, he asked, "Jalena Mathesin, will you be my wife? Will you marry me?"

She stood there. Lost for words, hesitating. As she stood there trying to understand what was taking place, she was in a state of disbelief that this was actually happening. She couldn't move or breathe.

"Jalena...will you?"

Breaking free from the paralyzing shock, she shouted, "Yes! Yes! I will. I will!"

Sage then stood up and placed the ring on her finger and they kissed. People were oohing and ahhing. Some clapped their hands and began congratulating them.

Jalena was overwhelmed by the proposal and also by the rush of complete strangers wanting to get in on what was happening. It was their special moment--their night. Seeing the gathered crowd getting larger, Sage rushed Jalena back into the limo where she rested in his arms.

Amazed at the ring he had placed on her finger, she held it out in front of her face, admiring the glistening shine that fell upon the crystals as the light of day touched its beauty. Sage poured Jalena a glass of champagne. With tear filled eyes, she said, "I can't wait for

Mom and Jared to see it and to hear the news!" Jalena was filled with joy and excitement.

"Mom already knows, J. She's already seen it."

"Sage!"

"Baby, I had to get her blessing. I wanted everything to be done the right way and in order. Can't have Mom mad at me, had to do it the biblically."

"Is that really in the Bible?"

"Oh, I don't know. But I'm glad I did; it just felt right."

"You were right to do so, but I still can't wait for her to see it on my hand!"

"Okay, but first we have dinner reservations at Citronelle in DC and then we'll head back to the house. My plan was to propose at the restaurant, but I'm glad things worked out this way; I just couldn't wait. I love you, babe," he said and kissed her.

"I love you, too, Sage. Thank you. I'll never forget this birthday for as long as I live. You've made me feel so special. I love you, Sage Linendoll, and I can't wait to be your wife." Jalena rested her head on his chest.

Chapter 42

Sage and Jalena had a wonderful dinner and then headed back home. As they walked into the house, everyone broke out into song, serenading Jalena with the birthday song adding a little bit of gospel flavor. Tahlia led them in the chorus. Family and friends gathered around, greeting Jalena and Sage as they walked through the room.

Although it was Jalena's birthday, Marinda was excited and broke the news about Jalena's engagement before they returned home from dinner. There were hugs and kisses for Jalena as she came in smiling and showing off her diamond engagement ring. Sage received handshakes and hugs from uncles, aunts and cousins. This was his first time meeting many of them. Uncle Raymond gave him the third degree and gentle warnings about the way Jalena was to be treated.

This was no longer about her birthday, but it was all about the engagement.

"Have you set the date?" was the question of the evening. After several answers of 'no', Jalena finally got everyone's attention and said, "Sage, I know we haven't discussed a date, but if it's okay with you, I'd like to set a date while here with our family and friends tonight."

Without hesitation he said, "Whatever you decide...the sooner the better." That response aroused quite a bit of laughter.

Looking over at Marinda, Jalena said, "Mom, do you remember the night I came home after being away from you and the family? Everyone knows how much of a mess I was when I was forced to leave the house. I can now say that it was the best thing that could have ever happened. It helped me grow up and become the woman that God purposed and planned for my life. I thank Him for covering me with His grace and mercy while I was out there on the streets, even though I was out of His will. He kept me safe, and I know that prayers were being lifted on my behalf. I felt it!"

Marinda softly said, "Yes, yes, yes...God answered my prayers!"

Jalena continued. "I thank God for you, Pastor Harvey and Greater Saint James Restoration Center for the many times I was able to have a hot meal and listen to the word. It changed me! Yes, it took time because in the beginning, I was totally resistant. But, I finally got it. I gave in to God and put aside all those things that were keeping me in bondage--drinking, the weed, but none of that matters to me anymore. The only thing that really matters to me right now is knowing that God truly loves me and that He's always watching over me. At first it was hard to even fathom the awesomeness of His love for me, but when I got it, it changed my life and who I was. I'm not the same."

Jalena was getting emotional as tears ran down her face with voice raised as if she were standing in a pulpit, preaching to the congregation. This was now her time. She had their attention. It was at this moment that she opened her mouth and freely declared her deliverance and salvation. It was also at this moment in time that she would tell those she loved standing around her about the magical dream she had - an encounter with God.

"Recently, in a dream I've had a couple of times, I was in heaven - floating among the clouds and dancing with God while a myriad of angels surrounded us. He spoke words of love, wisdom, encouragement and blessings in my ears. I've only told one other person about this dream. Tonight, I share that dream with you, my family and friends."

As she spoke in detail about the dream, they were enthralled by her words. There were tears shed and smiles on faces. These people surrounding her had endured the pain of her life along with Jalena, her Mom and Jared.

Wiping away tears, she said, "December 18th was the date I returned to this doorstep and Mom let me back into her heart and into this family. It's the date that will forever be engraved in my heart. And now, it will be the date that I'll walk down the aisle and give my heart and love to a man who loves me for who I am. It's our wedding date."

Jalena made her way to Sage and hugged him as he too, wiped away tears. He was overcome with emotion and didn't say a word, but nodded in agreement. She looked over at her mom, who was making her way to the couple. Wrapping her arms around her daughter, she tightly embraced her. At that moment, there was an outburst of applause and cheers along with more hugs and kisses. The atmosphere was one of celebrated joy. This would be the wedding to remember; the official date had been set.

Chapter 43

The weekend was over. Monday came quickly. The celebration was over, but the residue and feeling of joy still resided deep in Jalena's heart as she returned to work. She wished she had taken the day off, but knew there were important business concerns she needed to take care of. All morning Jalena watched the clock, waiting for Mr. Peters to enter. It was a late day at work for him, so he wouldn't get in until later in the day.

Her office colleagues surrounded Jalena's desk giving congratulations. Some even went downstairs to the gift shop and purchased engagement gifts. All of this was good, but Jalena remained distracted and was anxious to give the necklace back to Mr. Peters. Jalena knew it was the best thing to do. She hoped that he wouldn't take it to heart by firing her and using a bogus excuse to do so.

Jalena made up her mind not to worry. So she prayed. She knew that God had her back in any situation. This would be no exception.

Her original plan with Tahlia changed because of scheduling, so Tahlia dropped the necklace off to Jalena instead. Once she had it back in her hands, Jalena hid it carefully in the rear of her desk drawer. At noon, Mr. Peters entered the building. Jalena was happy that Laurie didn't work on Mondays, therefore, it made things easier for her to secretly return the gift.

As the clock ticked and time passed by, Jalena got nervous as she waited for him to make his regular visit to her side of the office. He finally appeared. With papers in hand, he took his spot on the corner of her desk.

Suavely he said, "Good morning, Jalena. Or should I say good afternoon?"

"Good afternoon, Mr. Peters."

Looking around to make sure the coast was clear, he softly said, "I'd like to finish the conversation we were having on Friday of last week. Did you think about anything that was said? You know...about going out?"

There was no hesitation. Without fear she said, "Oh, yes, I thought about it." She reached into her desk drawer while he continued talking.

"Jalena, as I said on Friday, I'd like to get to know you a little better by taking you out for dinner or lunch."

She swiftly handed him the box and said, "I cannot take this present you gave me."

"But, why?"

"Mr. Peters, first of all, you're my boss. Secondly, on Friday, I guess you hadn't noticed, but there were beautiful red roses in a crystal vase on my desk. They were sent special delivery by someone very dear to me. Mr. Peters, they were sent to me by the man that I truly love. I'm sorry, but I thought you knew."

"Whew! No, I didn't know."

Jalena then held out her hand and showed him her engagement ring and said, "Lastly, I'm engaged to be married to that man on December 18th. Mr. Peters, this diamond necklace that you gave me means nothing to me. I'm returning it to you so that you can either return it to Jared®'s Galleria or give it to your next prospective girlfriend."

Embarrassment and shame were written on his face.

"Jalena, I'm sorry for offending you. I didn't know you had someone special in your life. My sincere congratulations on your engagement. I lose...he wins. My procrastination caused me to forfeit dating the prettiest girl in the office."

Jalena felt that she had to ask Him a pertinent question. "Mr. Peters, is this going to cost me my job?"

Smiling, he answered, "Don't worry, we can still have a good working relationship. My heart is broken, but I'm good. Someone else will come along and steal my heart," he said as he stood to leave.

She sighed with relief.

"Well, young lady, get to work. We have that contract for Mrs. Davis that's due by midnight Wednesday." As he walked away, he said, "By the way, who's the lucky man? Do I know him?"

"No, I don't think you do. His name is Sage Linendoll."

"Linendoll? Linendoll...Sage Linendoll....where have I heard that name before? Sounds quite familiar to me. Hmm...ok...well, anyway...he's a very lucky man. Now get to work."

Jalena was happy she set the record straight with Mr. Peters. Joy would last after all.

Walking into his business suite, Jonathan Peters stopped cold in his tracks. Looking at his Executive Secretary, he was deep in thought as his memory cleared.

"Myra."

"Yes, Mr. Peters, did you need something?"

"I do. Where's the file we had for a Mr. Sage Linendoll? Is it here or at headquarters?"

"It's here, Mr. Peters. As a matter of fact, I just pulled it for a revision that he wants to make to his will."

"Bring it to me, please."

"Yes, sir, right away."

"Mr. Sage Linendoll? I knew that name sounded familiar," he said aloud.

As he sat at his desk, Myra laid the file down in front of him.

"That was quick. Thanks, Myra."

"You're welcome, Sir."

He quickly opened the file folder and began perusing each document.

"Hmm...okay...okay. Jalena Mathesin, you're one rich, lucky lady. Wait until you find out how truly blessed you are. I guess I'd better start looking for someone to take over your position quickly," he said shaking his head. Sadness slowly revealed itself upon his face.

Chapter 44

Mrs. Marinda Mathesin & Ms. Cora Bergman
request the honor of your presence
at the marriage of their children
Jalena Marinda Mathesin
&
Sage Benjamin Linendoll
Saturday, the eighteenth of December
Two thousand and fourteen
four o'clock in the afternoon
at the New Hope Baptist Church
2515 Everly Avenue - Fort Washington, MD
Reception to follow

The wedding was small but elegantly tasteful. Family and friends came together at the Church where Jalena grew up and where most of her family were united. Her uncle and aunt even came from Florida to take part in the grand occasion.

Jalena requested that everyone attending should wear white to the affair. When walking down the small aisle of the church, there was nothing but a sea of white, just like the angels in heaven. Her bridesmaids wore red, while the groomsmen wore white tuxedos with red accessories. Jared was Sages best man, and Sasha was the junior bridesmaid. Jalena wanted no arguments between her two friends, so she made Tahlia and Sharina her maids of honor.

Since the dream of dancing with God was always in her mind and she remembered the dress she wore in heaven, Jalena's gown was made to match that memory. It was a simple, white dress with short ruffled sleeves, scoop neck bodice and a taffeta skirt with a long red ribbon tied at her waist.

Everyone admired how beautiful a bride she was. Most commented that they could see a glow on her face as she entered the sanctuary through the double glass doors. Tears of joy streamed down Jalena's face when she saw all her friends and loved ones, resembling angels dressed in their white. All had been a part of her life from birth. Now they were here as witnesses her newness of life--a place that God had sanctioned and purposed for her. Jalena could see and feel the love from each one as she walked down the aisle. There were tears of joy flowing from some, including her mother.

Sitting on n a wooden chair next to Marinda was a gold framed photo of Jalena's dad. There was also a picture of Sages parents on a chair between his Aunt Cora and his neighbor from Illinois, Ms. Bethany Willsworth. Traditional vows of love and honor were exchanged as the two of them were bonded together under a floral trellis filled with red and white roses. Elder Joseph England, Jalena's second cousin, officiated and helped the couple to set sail on their journey of love in marriage.

"I now pronounce you husband and wife. Mr. Sage Linendoll, you may now kiss your bride," he said with a smile.

As they kissed, applause erupted with shouts of exuberant joy and excitement. Cameras flashed all around them.

The elder then said, "Friends and family, I now introduce to you, for the first time, Mr. and Mrs. Sage Benjamin Linendoll."

The organist began to play as the happy couple jumped the broom and made their way down the aisle among the cheering congregation.

<>><>

When they danced for the first time as husband and wife at the reception in the church fellowship hall, Jalena closed her eyes and for a moment thought she was floating on air once again dancing with God -- the King of King and Lord of Lords.

Dressed in white, her family and friends surrounded them like the heavenly angels on the dance floor of heaven. It was a great image.

As they danced, Sage whispered in her ear. At one point, Jalena thought she could actually hear the voice of God speaking to her. Blocking out everything else around her, Jalena held magical those images that were dear to her heart within her mind.

With every step they took, she knew in her heart that God alone was the wedding planner and that it was all a part of His purposed plan for her tested life. Her entire life had been truly a dance with God--no more street life, the drugs, hardship and pain that she once knew and lived. Now, life was a place of love, peace and joy as she floated on air, dancing with the man that God had gifted her. She was glad to have the honor, privilege and pleasure to be one of the few chosen to dance with God.

Epilogue

Away on their honeymoon, Jalena lay awake with eyes on her husband and thought these words:

As I lie here next to him, I can't help but watch him as he sleeps. Silently I wait and as I wait for his awakening, I wonder and dream of the plans he has for me. He promised me so many things on our wedding day. He said he would love me till death do us part and give me every desire of my heart. When we danced our first dance, he whispered his undying love for me and made me blush with every step we took as the musicians played our favorite tunes. He was brought to tears when he spoke of his parents and my dad, wishing they were here with us on our special day.

How can he love me? How can anyone love me the way that he does after knowing the kind of life I have lived? Love is an action word, and he has acted upon his love for me since the first day we met. At first he caught me off guard with the way he was acting, so suave and debonair. Then he sneaked and snipped a rose for me in our horticulture class. How could I refuse his flirting, especially after the teacher found out and gave him detention.

This is the love of a lifetime; it's a love that will last forever. His love emulates the love that God has for me. I truly believe he would give his life for me if he had to. I love my Sage. Thank you, Father God for sending your love through this gift you have given me in Sage Linendoll. Now sleep, my love. I'll patiently wait for you here by your loving side.

Psalm 139:13-16

For you created my inmost being; you knit me together in my mother's womb. I praise you because I am fearfully and wonderfully made; your works are wonderful, I know that full well. My frame was not hidden from you when I was made in the secret place. When I was woven together in the depths of the earth, your eyes saw my unformed body. All the days ordained for me were written in your book before one of them came to be.

Thanks for reading! If you enjoyed this book or found it inspirational, I'd be very grateful if you'd post a short review on Amazon.com. Your support really does make a difference and I read all the reviews personally. Thanks again for your support!

Theresa M. Odom-Surgick